She'd been seen.

Somebody was there.

Jody could just make out a dark form, motionless in the snow. Standing there.

Staring.

Staring up at *her*.

Jody suddenly shrank back and ducked down, her heart pounding like a drum. She'd been seen. The glass in the binoculars must have caught the moonlight and given her away. And now, whoever was out there knew Jody had been watching everything.

**Other Point paperbacks
you will enjoy:**

point

THE WINDOW

Carol Ellis

SCHOLASTIC INC.

New York Toronto London Auckland Sydney

ISBN 0-590-44916-8

12 11 10 9 8 7 6 5 4 3   2 3 4 5 6 7/9

Printed in the U.S.A.   01

First Scholastic printing, January 1992

THE WINDOW

Chapter 1

Jody Sanderson closed her eyes, but it didn't help. The van had just hit a patch of ice and was sliding to the right. It veered across the frozen surface toward the safety rail separating the highway from a rocky gorge forty feet below. In her mind's eye, Jody watched the silver-gray van gliding almost gracefully across the ice, bursting through the flimsy rail, and soaring into the air where it hung suspended for a few seconds, streamlined and glinting in the pale sun. Before she could picture its terrifying, deadly plunge toward the rocks, Jody felt the tires regain their traction. Releasing the breath she'd been holding, Jody felt her body lean with the van as it pulled left, back toward the safety of the highway.

Jody opened her eyes and looked around. No one else in the van seemed to have suffered from the same flight of imagination she had. In the seat across from her, Christine Castella was still holding her paperback, although the main focus of her attention was obviously Drew Hansen, across and up one seat. Jody couldn't blame Chris for not concentrating on her book; Drew was very good-looking, in a brown-eyed, brooding sort of way. He'd attracted the attention of Ellen Cummings, too, Jody'd noticed earlier. All Jody could see of Ellen at the moment was the top of her light-brown hair above the seatback ahead, but she was willing to bet that Ellen was staring at the seat across from *her*, wishing hard that Drew would turn and talk to her.

Behind her, Jody could hear the sound of Billy Feldman's even, slightly stuffy breathing. If he was asleep, then he hadn't noticed how close they'd come to disaster, and if he was awake, then it must not have bothered him in the slightest.

It hadn't bothered the driver of the van, either, Jody noticed. Sasha Wolf, her long dark hair spilling down her back in shining waves, turned her head to the side just long enough for Jody to see that she was smiling. Her twin brother, Cal, smiled back.

"They're beautiful," Jody's friend Kate had said of her neighbors, the Wolf twins. After meeting them earlier that morning, Jody had agreed. Tall and slender, dark-haired and blue-eyed, Sasha and Cal Wolf were beautiful, all right. Whether Sasha was a good enough driver to keep them alive the rest of the three-hour drive to Brevard Pass remained to be seen.

Scrunching down in her seat, Jody told herself that she really didn't know any of these people well enough to be making judgments about them. She had to give them a chance. Still, she wished Kate had been able to come on the ski trip. After all, *Kate* was the one who'd invited her. Sasha and Cal had rented the cabin, and invited Kate, who in turn had invited Jody. But now Kate was sick with the flu, and Jody was stuck with a bunch of strangers.

Well, they weren't *all* strangers. She knew Billy and Chris a little from school. Billy was kind of a klutz, that's all she really knew about him. But Chris, with her spiky blonde hair and blue eyes that always stared at the air above your head, was *not* the kind of person Jody was dying to spend five days in a cabin with.

But as Kate said when she'd called the night before to say good-bye, this wasn't just any ski trip. This was Brevard Pass, *the* place to go skiing. Jody couldn't pass it up. Besides, Kate said she *needed* Jody to go. Leahna Calder was going to be there. Jody had never heard of Leahna Calder. Kate said she was poison. She said she needed Jody to keep an eye on Cal and let Kate know if Leahna started sinking her claws into him.

Jody grinned to herself. Kate had told her at least a thousand times how she'd die for Cal Wolf, and from her first look at him, Jody couldn't blame her. But she had no intention of keeping an eye on Cal and Leahna. This was a ski trip, not an undercover assignment.

The last thing Kate had said the night before was not to worry about not knowing anyone, that she'd have a great time. Now, as the van barreled along the highway, Jody looked around and tried to decide if these were people she could have a great time with. When they skidded across another patch of ice, Jody closed her eyes again. With Sasha's driving, she'd be lucky if she got the chance to find out.

About forty miles later, the highway narrowed from four lanes to two. Looking out the window, Jody saw a small white sign bordered in dark green. Black lettering announced that Brevard Pass was ten miles away.

"Brevard Pass," Billy said from the seat behind her, obviously having seen the sign, too. "It used to be just what it says, a plain old mountain pass used by wagons. Named after Charles Brevard. He was the first guy to cross it, back in 1852, something like that."

"Thanks for the history lesson," Chris said.

Jody twisted around and looked at Billy. "This is my first time here," she told him. "It's so popular, I guess I expected bells and whistles. Or at least a bigger sign."

"Neon?" Chris asked sarcastically, never taking her eyes off Drew.

"Just bigger." Jody decided her snap impression of Chris had been right on the mark. The girl's personality was as spiky as her hair.

"I know what you mean, Jody." Sasha took her eyes off the road and smiled warmly in the rearview mirror. Her voice was low and throaty. "You hear so much about Brevard, you expect bells and whistles, like you said. I think the people who live here all year-round didn't want it to turn into another Aspen."

"But that's what it is, almost," Billy said. "It's got night skiing, it's got a lodge that looks like a mansion, it's got famous people buying up land and spending millions."

"Yes, but it's not flashy." Sasha peered at him in the mirror. "Brevard's got class."

"Okay. Just as long as it's got snow, too." Billy laughed a little too loudly at his small joke. His liquid brown eyes reminded Jody of a puppy's. The poor guy, she thought, he's got a thing for Sasha. She hoped he realized he'd probably have to wait in line.

"There'll be plenty of snow," Ellen said seriously. Her voice was airy and kind of singsongy. "I listened to the weather report this morning and Brevard got two inches last night. The base is packed, and it's almost eighty inches, they said."

Sasha and Cal exchanged another quick smile. Jody could almost hear them saying, "Great! The slopes are going to be perfect." At least that's what she imagined they might be saying. The two of them seemed to communicate without words half the time. Kate said they were really close, being twins and all. Jody supposed it was normal, considering, but it made her feel a little left out. Why couldn't they talk out loud, like everybody else?

As if he felt her watching him, Cal turned around in his seat and looked down the aisle toward Jody. His light-blue eyes were sparkling. "Kate told us you're a pretty good skier," he said. "Are you ready for the Jaws of Death?"

"The *what*?"

"He means one of the runs." Drew's dark-blond head appeared over the rim of his seat. "The hard one."

"Drew!" Sasha called out. She lifted her hand and waved, a wide silver bracelet shining on her wrist. "I was wondering when you'd surface. Have you been asleep or were you just sunk in one of your moody spells?"

"Neither, Sasha. I was praying we wouldn't go off the highway whenever you didn't bother to slow down for the ice." Drew's head sank down behind his seatback again.

Jody grinned. At least one person was on her wavelength.

Sasha laughed, strong and full. "You should have told me you were worried, Drew. I would have slowed down if I'd known."

"That would have spoiled the thrill," Drew's disembodied voice said.

Sasha laughed again. "Was anybody else scared?" she asked. "Come on, you can tell me. If you were, I'll let Cal drive on the trip back home. He's much more cautious than I am."

"I don't even want to think about the trip back," Chris whined. "We've been in this van forever, it feels like. Are we almost there?"

"About five more minutes." Cal pointed out the window to where several long lines of almost identical A-frame cabins were strung along a snowy hillside dotted with pine trees. "We're in one of those. Which row, Sash, the third?"

"Mmm, the third. Cabins above and below us,"

Sasha said. "Big windows and no curtains. Don't walk naked to the shower . . . unless you *like* being watched," she added.

Jody thought that was sort of an odd thing to say. But everyone else laughed, Billy the loudest. "I'd rather *do* the watching," he said. "Anybody bring binoculars?"

"Who'd want to spend their time staring into windows?" Ellen asked. "We came to ski."

"There's always nighttime," Chris reminded her. "Unless you plan to ski then, too."

"Oh, sure I do." Ellen's voice got higher and much more animated. "That's the most beautiful time."

"Yeah," Drew murmured. "Down the slopes in the moonlight. Nothing better."

"There's more floodlight than moonlight, but I know what you mean," Sasha said. "No skiing tonight, though." She glanced at Cal.

"I knew it!" Cal laughed. "You set it up, didn't you?"

"I told you I would."

"Set what up?" Billy draped himself over the back of Jody's seat. "Set what up, Sasha?"

Cal answered him. "Party time, my friend. Sasha's been on the phone all week, talking to everybody we know who'll be here."

"Most of them are coming, too, and we'll invite a bunch more this afternoon. Whoever looks interesting and fun," Sasha said. "The main lodge does five-foot submarine sandwiches — I'll order a couple as soon as we get to the cabin. It'll be perfect."

"It'll be wild," Cal added.

"Oh, definitely wild," Sasha agreed. "So everybody save the moonlit slopes for another night."

"Do we have a choice?" Drew asked.

Chris snickered.

Jody saw a small frown flit across Sasha's face, but it disappeared quickly, and she laughed. "I was doing it again, wasn't I, Cal?"

"Mmm." He turned around and grinned at the rest of the passengers. "Sasha's into taking charge, in case nobody could tell."

"I get a little pushy sometimes," Sasha admitted. "*Of course* you don't have to be at the party, Drew." She eyed him in the mirror, her beautiful face slightly flushed. "It's strictly voluntary."

"Good, I'm glad we've got that straight." Drew subsided again, and Jody thought he was finished talking. Then he added, "A party sounds fine. Count me in, Sasha."

"I never seriously counted you out," Sasha told him with a grin, and Jody heard Drew laugh for the first time.

"Hey, we're here!" Billy called out as they passed a sign welcoming them to Brevard Pass. "Look, there's the lift."

Off to the right, Jody saw the lift moving slowly up the mountainside, the skiers' jackets bright splashes of color against the snow beneath them. She watched excitedly, as Sasha pulled the van into the parking area at the base of the cabin-dotted hill.

It was almost noon. Nobody wanted to unload and waste time trekking with their bags to the cabin; everyone wanted to get on the slopes. But leaving everything in the van, even if it was locked, wasn't such a great idea.

"I'll carry the stuff," Drew volunteered as they all piled out of the van. "I want to check out the cabin."

"Third row, remember," Sasha said. "You'll see the number eight on the deck railing. That's the one." There were keys for everyone staying at the cabin, and she tossed Drew's to him. "And could you call the lodge and order the subs for tonight? And be sure to turn up the heat?"

"I'll help, too," Chris said, flashing a smile at Drew. "I'm going to need to go into town before I can start skiing, anyway. My dog chewed up my best gloves last night, and I have to buy another pair." She held up her hands. Her arms jingled with bracelets, and every finger except her thumbs had a ring on it.

"You'll both get rewards," Cal told them. "I don't know what, but we'll think of something."

"How about if you pay for our lift tickets?" Drew suggested.

Cal laughed. "How about if I carry my own bags, instead?"

Drew laughed, too, shaking his head. Then he turned to the van and started lifting the skis off the top.

The joking around helped Jody feel loose for the first time since the trip had started. She reminded herself that she probably wasn't the only one who'd been uncomfortable; they'd all been circling each other a little, trying to feel each other out, deciding if they could be friends, or at least stand each other for the five days they'd be at Brevard.

"Who's got the Heads?" Drew asked, propping a pair of skis against the van.

"I do." Jody finished pulling on her ski pants and walked over to him. "Thanks." She pulled out her wallet, took the money she'd need for the lift ticket, and handed the wallet to him.

"You sure you trust me with this?" Drew asked seriously.

Jody grinned. "I trusted Sasha to get us here in one piece, didn't I?"

Drew laughed and leaned his head close to Jody's. "I guess Cal's got your vote to drive back," he said softly.

Jody nodded, enjoying the conspiracy. Enjoying his closeness, too.

"That makes two of us," he said. "Let's try to talk the others into coming over to our side. Deal?"

"Deal." Jody laughed, then reached past him to take her skis. As she turned around, she saw that Chris was watching her. All Jody's good feelings froze like the hard-packed snow under her feet. Chris's face was a mask of hate.

Chapter 2

Riding up in the lift, Jody breathed deeply, taking in a great gulp of the cold air. She kept telling herself she'd only imagined the hatred in Chris's eyes. Chris was probably just squinting in the sun, and that always distorted people's faces. Still, Jody couldn't help feeling that Chris wanted Drew for herself, and thought Jody was butting into her territory.

Jody shivered as she watched the skiers below making their runs. She was anxious to get off the lift and join them. Thinking about Chris's look bothered her, like remembering a bad dream. Once Jody was up on the slopes, she could forget about Chris and just think about skiing, which she loved.

In a couple of minutes, the lift had reached the top. Jody stood up and slid down the snow-covered, wooden ramp. Then she poled on a few feet farther, where most of the people were heading, toward the intermediate slopes. Once there, she checked her bindings, then maneuvered herself into position.

Just before she pulled down her goggles, she saw Ellen, looking very pretty in pale blue, get off the lift. Behind her came Sasha and Cal. Sasha was wearing red and black, very dramatic, Jody thought. It made her own teal and yellow seem washed out, but Jody figured Sasha probably made most girls feel washed out. She wondered if Cal, long and lean in black and silver, had the same effect on guys.

But Jody didn't stand around wondering for long. There was a whole afternoon of skiing ahead. She still hadn't decided whether she could have a great time with these people, but she knew she could enjoy the slopes. She pulled down her goggles, jabbed her poles into the snow, and pushed off down the slope.

An hour later, Jody came to a perfect stop at the bottom of the slope, slid up her goggles and grinned to herself. This one had been her best run yet; she'd felt completely in control, her body doing exactly what it was supposed to do.

Exhilirated, her cheeks tingling, Jody glanced up the slope and tried not to laugh. Here came Billy, floundering in the powder, his legs straight as sticks. Jody felt like shouting at him to bend his knees, but he was too far away. She covered her eyes, then slid her fingers apart and watched as Billy came up over a small rise. His body was ramrod straight, and his poles were dragging. He didn't stand a chance.

Jody covered her eyes again, cringing in sympathy for what she knew was coming. When she finally looked, Billy was spitting snow and trying to pick himself up from a tangle of skis and poles.

Once he got himself together, he trudged down the rest of the way and stopped in front of Jody, breathing heavily.

"That *was* the Jaws of Death, wasn't it?" he asked.

Jody laughed. "I hate to tell you . . ."

"I know, I know. I belong on the beginners' slope," Billy said. He brushed more snow off his hair. "It's too humiliating, though. Some of those kids in grade school are better than I am."

"I guess I'd feel the same way. You've probably heard this before, but you should bend your knees, go into a sort of semi-crouch." Jody found herself cringing again: Billy's lips were chapped, and his forehead and nose were sunburned. "And wear some sunscreen," she added. "Your face is going to be sore."

"Yeah? That'll be nothing, compared to the way the rest of me feels already." He started putting his skis back on. "Give me a minute, okay? I'll walk over to the lift with you."

"You're going up again?"

"You're surprised? I don't blame you." Billy was tightening his bindings, his goggles dangling from one ear.

"Well, a little," Jody admitted. "But at least you don't quit."

"That's not it. I have a reputation to keep up." The goggles plopped into the snow, and he got his skis crossed shuffling around to pick them up.

"Don't move," Jody said. She bent easily, got the goggles, and held them out to him. "What do you mean, a reputation?"

"I'm the laugh man," he said as they headed for the lift line. "I either tell jokes or — "

"Or what?"

"Or I *am* the joke." Billy's smile had faded, and, for an instant, Jody thought he looked almost angry. "Haven't you figured that out?" he asked.

Jody shook her head, embarrassed. "We hardly know each other," she reminded him. "What about the others? Do they know you really well?"

"Nope." Billy looked at her. "Why'd you ask that? No, wait, I know. You're saying I could make a new image for myself, become a new Billy Feldman, at least while we're here?"

"No, but now that you mention it, I guess you could," Jody said. "I mean, if you wanted to." She bet he wanted to, especially with Sasha. Jody felt funny giving him advice. Besides, she didn't think he stood a chance with Sasha Wolf, no matter what kind of new image he came up with.

They were at the lift line by now, but suddenly Billy shuffled to the side. "On second thought, I think I'll sit out for a while, anyway, give myself a break. See you later, Jody."

There's definitely more to him than that clownish image he puts on, Jody thought. Just before she got on the lift, she turned around and looked at Billy. He was standing where she'd left him, watching a skier coming down the slope. A skier in dramatic red and black with perfect form and dark, gleaming hair whipping out behind her. It was Sasha. Billy gaped up at her, his skis pigeon-toed. Jody hoped he remembered to straighten them out and close his mouth before Sasha reached him.

By late afternoon, the sky had clouded over and a few snowflakes were whirling around in the wind. Jody came out of one of the warm-up huts, where she'd just gulped down some hot chocolate, and tried to decide whether to go back up. A nice warm cabin, a hot shower, and a change of clothes were tempting. Maybe one more run, she decided. Then she'd call it quits for the day.

She hadn't seen Drew or Chris since she'd left them at the van earlier, but when she got off the lift, she saw both of them at the top of the ridge. In fact, the entire group was there.

"Jody!" Sasha called out as Jody slid toward them. "Come on, you're just in time!"

"For what?"

"Sasha just had a brilliant idea," Cal said. "Well, *she* thinks it's brilliant. I think it's a little crazy, myself."

"Come on!" Sasha gave her brother a light punch on the arm. "You love it, I can tell." She tossed her head and laughed. "You're just scared you won't be able to do it."

"I *know* I won't be able to do it," Cal said.

"Do what?" Jody asked.

Ellen touched her lightly on the arm. "Look down the slope," she said, pointing with her pole. "There's that bunch of trees and then there's a little rise. What do you see?"

Blinking the snowflakes off her eyelashes, Jody squinted down the slope. At first she didn't see anything but snow. Then, just past a group of pines, she thought she saw a small rock. It was awfully bright for a rock, though. "I give up," she said. "What is it?"

"An orange peel," Ellen said.

"Okay," Jody laughed. "What's the brilliant idea?"

"A contest," Sasha said excitedly. "You have to ski down, stab the orange peel with your pole, go around the trees and then over the rise. The run flattens out for a few yards after that and there's a place where you can stop, so you don't have to go all the way down. Whoever makes the fastest time wins."

"Whoever makes it down *alive*, you mean," Cal said. "You'll be coming around the trees, there's no time to stab an orange peel and get set for the rise. Your balance will be all wrong."

"Oh, come on," Sasha said. "It'll be fun!"

"Great," Chris muttered, completely without enthusiasm. "An orange-peel slalom."

"All you have to do is holler when you've stopped." Sasha walked over next to Billy and threw her arm around his shoulders. "Billy, you'd like to be our timekeeper, wouldn't you?" She pulled off her watch and handed it to him. "It works as a stopwatch, too," she explained, pointing to a little button on the side.

Billy took the watch, his face even redder than it had been earlier. Probably because Sasha was so close, Jody thought. "Sure, Sasha," he said. "I'll keep time for you."

"Smart man, Billy," Cal said. "Good way to get out of it."

"Hey, somebody's gotta punch the button," Billy said with a grin. "Besides, I defy anybody to equal my finesse with a stopwatch."

"Well, come on, you guys!" Sasha urged. "Drew, don't you want to try?"

Jody wasn't sure Drew had been listening. He hadn't greeted her when she arrived, and even though Chris had planted herself right next to him, Drew hadn't said a word to her, either. While the rest of them had been discussing the orange-peel slalom, he'd been staring off into the distance.

Jody wondered if he thought this whole thing sounded dangerous, like she did. Skiing around the trees and getting set for the rise was hard enough. Trying to stab an orange peel could make you shift your balance so much that you'd come over the rise all wrong. If you landed badly, you might do more than just take a spill.

Or was there something else bothering Drew, Jody wondered.

"Drew?" Sasha said again. She sounded excited and a little impatient. This was her idea, Jody thought; she wanted everyone to think it was as great as she did.

"Why don't you go first, Sasha?" Chris sneered a little.

"We could draw straws," Billy suggested, when Sasha didn't say anything to Chris. "Well, not straws. How about pine needles?"

Sasha ignored him. "*Of course* I'll go first," she said, pulling down her goggles and getting into position. "I *expected* to go first." She looked over at her brother, and Jody saw that Cal was already getting ready to go next. She couldn't tell if he'd decided on his own or if Sasha had somehow egged him on without saying a word. Or maybe he was just silently sticking by her.

Drew finally spoke up. "Don't get all bent out of shape, Sasha. Most of us just hadn't planned on breaking a leg our first day out, that's all."

Sasha smiled around the group. "Nobody *has* to go, really. I'm sorry if I got pushy again." With that, she was off, down the slope and around the trees. She missed the orange peel, kept going, and a moment later they heard her call out, "Come on, Cal!"

"Here goes nothing." Cal took off in a flash of silver and black. His form was as good as Sasha's, but he didn't get the orange peel, either.

The snow was coming down more heavily now, and not many other skiers were up on the slopes. Billy reset the stopwatch. "Okay, who's next?"

Chris sighed loudly. "I just want to get this over with," she said, stomping into position. "Don't bother to time me, Billy. I'm not even going to try for the dumb orange peel."

But at the last minute, coming around the trees, Chris must have changed her mind. She swung her right pole out toward the orange peel and jabbed down.

"Hey!" Billy shouted. "I think she got it!"

But the rise was coming up fast, and Chris had to shift her weight back to the left to be ready for it. She bent her knees, leaned left, and brought her right pole back to tuck it under her arm. She took the rise in good shape, but she left the orange peel about a foot farther to the right than it had been.

Drew looked at Jody. "She just gave us the perfect excuse not to try for the orange peel."

"That's what I was thinking," Jody laughed.

"Yeah?" His dark-brown eyes flickered over her face, and he smiled a little. "Looks like we're on the same wavelength again."

Jody watched him push off, feeling a little excited. He was awfully good-looking, and when he wasn't being quiet and moody, he seemed really nice. She wasn't going out with anybody right now, but she hadn't come on the trip to find a guy. Still, if something started to happen between her and Drew, she might have trouble resisting.

Remembering that Ellen had seemed interested in Drew, too, Jody stopped grinning to herself and glanced at her. Ellen wasn't shooting her a look that could kill, at least. She just looked sad. Ellen was thin, almost frail-looking, and the disappointment in her soft hazel eyes gave Jody a twinge. But the twinge didn't last long. She didn't know Ellen, she didn't really know Drew, she didn't even know if he was interested in her or not. And she wasn't going to get all upset worrying about it.

"Do you want to go now, or shall I?" she asked.

"I'll go." Ellen dug in her poles and pushed off. Jody hadn't seen her ski before now. Jody was surprised to learn that for somebody so frail-looking, Ellen was smooth and strong and sure of herself.

"What about you?" Jody asked Billy. "Can you get down okay?"

"Oh, sure, I'll make it. I'll hike down if I have to."

Jody laughed and pushed off, not even glancing at the orange peel as she came around the trees. She took the rise and landed a little shakily, but managed to keep her balance. The run flattened out, as Sasha had said, and a few yards away, Jody saw the group waiting for her.

Jody heard laughter as she came to a stop; even Chris had a smile on her face. Somebody should tell her to smile more often, Jody thought. It was a refreshing change from the prickly look she usually wore.

"I don't know what happened to me," Chris was saying. "When I started, I was just going to ignore the orange peel, but then I couldn't resist taking a stab at it."

"How far away is it now?" Cal asked Jody.

"Too far," Jody laughed.

"We can always move it back," Sasha suggested.

"Well, it's snowing too hard now, anyway," Cal said. "Let's wait for Billy and go to the cabin. My toes are numb."

"Right, my face feels like a slab of ice," Drew said. "I could use something hot to drink. Where is Billy, anyway?"

Jody started to say it might take him a while to get down, but just then, a skier appeared over the rise. For a second, she thought it was Billy, but she changed her mind fast. The skier looked like an ad for the best in style and form: bright white outfit with neon-green stripes, knees bent perfectly to absorb the impact of the landing. Besides, this skier was a girl. Thick, taffy-colored hair swirled out behind her as she dug in her poles and pushed toward them.

"Look, I don't believe it!" Chris said. "She's got the orange peel!"

Sure enough, as the skier lifted her left pole and waved it triumphantly, everyone could see the glistening orange peel stuck to the end of it.

"Hey, is that who I think it is?" Cal said.

Drew's expression hardened, and he frowned at the skier. "Couldn't be anybody else," he said, his voice tight.

"Who?" Chris asked.

"It's Leahna," Ellen said softly.

"Yeah. Leahna." Cal breathed out her name on a sigh.

Leahna Calder. Jody suddenly felt very sorry for Kate. From the look on Cal's face, he was more than just "interested" in Leahna. He was crazy about her.

Chapter 3

Thawed out from a hot shower, Jody left the bathroom and padded up the open-tread stairs to the cabin's second floor. It was dark out now, and remembering Sasha's comment about the windows, Jody kept a tight hold on the king-size bath towel she'd wrapped around herself.

Reaching the second floor, she stopped and looked over the railing, down to the living room below. The floor was wood, scattered over with American-Indian-type rugs. The chairs and couch were covered in bright blue corduroy, and a fire was burning in an orange, free-standing fireplace. Underneath where she was standing, was the kitchen, gleaming white and modern. The place had everything, right down to extra goggles and toothpaste. All they'd had to bring was food.

Jody knew from Kate that the owners were friends of Cal's and Sasha's parents, which was why they'd gotten a nice break on the rent. Thank God for that, she thought. She'd never have been able to afford whatever they charged strangers.

As she was turning to go into the girls' half of the upstairs sleeping loft, Jody saw a movement out of the corner of her eye. She looked back down and saw Sasha stride into the living room from the back of the cabin. She was carrying two wooden bowls, one each of chips and pretzels, which she set down on the coffee table. Behind her came Cal, his arms full of logs for the fireplace.

Sasha dropped onto the couch and stretched her long legs out. "Listen," she said.

"I did. I don't want to listen anymore." Cal dumped the logs into a brass holder and walked out.

Jody followed his dark head until it disappeared, then she looked back at the couch. Sasha was sitting up now, staring at the fire. Jody couldn't see her face, but from the way Sasha's shoulders were hunched, she knew she wasn't happy.

Trouble in twinland, Jody thought. The two of them seemed like such perfect soulmates, it was almost reassuring to see that they could argue, just like a normal brother and sister.

In spite of the closeness that shut everyone out sometimes, Jody liked them. Sasha tried to take over a lot, but she was so charming when somebody called her on it, you couldn't hold it against her. And Cal was even better: looser, funnier, and really sexy. Jody might have been interested in him herself, but after watching him practically drool over Leahna Calder earlier, she figured everyone else's romantic chances with him were close to zero.

Not wanting to get caught staring, Jody turned away and went down the hall that divided the two big sleeping lofts, frowning as she thought of Drew's reaction to Leahna. He'd looked angry at her, but he hadn't been able to take his eyes off her, either. It was almost as if he couldn't decide whether he loved her or hated her.

Chris was in the girls' half of the loft, stretched out on the floor with a magazine. Jody stepped over pillows and duffel bags and went to the end by the window, where she'd dumped her stuff on one of the low beds.

"Is Ellen in the shower now?" Chris asked.

"Mmm. She said she wouldn't be long." Jody pulled on jeans and a pink wool sweater, sitting on the floor to do it. Sasha hadn't been kidding about no curtains. The window was big, too, covering almost the whole end of the room. Standing up, Jody looked out and up, right into the brightly lit window of the cabin above theirs. A figure crossed the room, and Jody turned away. Then she laughed.

"What?" Chris asked, licking her fingertip to turn the magazine page.

"I just noticed those binoculars," Jody said, pointing to a pair hanging by their leather strap from a hook on the back of the door. "They must belong to the owners. I saw somebody in the cabin out there and actually wanted to get a better look." She laughed again. "I sound like Billy."

"Umm." Chris turned another page, then glanced at Jody. "What did you think of the Lovely Leahna?"

Uh-oh, Jody thought. She wasn't sure she wanted to get into this conversation. "Well, she

. . ." Jody rubbed her hair with the towel and tried to think of something diplomatic to say. "She's a good skier."

Chris laughed. "Right. She's also gorgeous and rich and spoiled rotten."

"You know her?"

"I've met her a few times. She goes to the same school with Cal and Sasha and Drew and Ellen." Chris flipped the magazine aside and stood up, stretching. "Cal's obviously wild for her, but I was hoping Drew was smarter than that."

Jody sat on the bed and started combing her hair. "What do you mean?"

"I mean, Drew and Leahna were seeing each other for a while," Chris said. "He was crazy for her, and I guess while it lasted, it really sizzled." She snorted. "Of course, it didn't last long. Nothing ever lasts long with Leahna."

"What happened?"

"What do you think?" Chris asked. "She dropped him. She got him to where he couldn't think about anything but her, and then she told him to get lost."

"Why?"

"Because," Chris said impatiently, "that's what she likes to do — play with people's feelings. From what I heard, it was a pretty ugly scene — Drew shouted at her and called her every name in the book, told her she'd be sorry some day."

Remembering Drew's reaction to Leahna on the slopes, Jody's heart sank a little. He probably *did* hate her, she thought. But he certainly wasn't over her.

"Anyway," Chris went on, "like I said, I was hoping Drew had gotten smart. But I'll bet he's down in the kitchen right now, trying to get Leahna on the phone to invite her to the party again." Chris obviously didn't care much about the windows. She undressed in the middle of the room and walked casually to the bed where she'd flung her robe. "Didn't you hear him and Cal inviting her before?"

Jody shook her head. "I saw them talking to her, but they were too far away for me to hear."

"Well, I heard them." Chris tossed her head and changed her voice. " 'A party sounds wonderful, but I don't know. I might be flying to Antigua tomorrow, and I'll need to get to bed early.' Antigua, can you believe it?" Chris said in her own voice. "I wish she was there right now."

"Well, maybe she will be tomorrow," Jody said. "Then you can . . ." she stopped, but Chris picked up on it.

"I can go after Drew again?" she asked. "Yes, I plan to. The question is, will I be the only one?" Chris eyed Jody, a small smile on her lips.

It was a challenge, Jody knew it. She was tempted to say something, but the thought of exchanging nasty remarks with Chris was really kind of disgusting.

Chris was still watching her. The look in her eyes made Jody nervous, so she got up and started rummaging through her duffel bag for some eye makeup.

"I probably won't be the only one," Chris said,

answering her own question. "Ellen's been hanging around him as much as possible. I don't think I have to worry about *her*, though. But I'll have to keep my eye on Leahna." She laughed a little. "What about you, Jody?"

Chris's tone still made Jody nervous, but she could feel herself starting to get mad, too. She slammed down the little eye-shadow compact and took a deep breath. "No, I'm not worried about Leahna," she said. "I'll leave that to you. I'm sure you can handle it."

"Yeah?" Chris laughed again, maliciously. "So am I."

Ellen came into the room then, bundled in a thick white bathrobe and carrying a telephone. "Jody, your friend Kate's on the phone," she said, looking around for the wall plug. "Cal found this extension in one of the kitchen cabinets, so you can talk up here."

Ellen found the plug and hooked up the phone, and Chris gathered up her shampoo and conditioner and left the room. Jody settled on her bed and picked up the receiver. "Hi, how are you feeling?"

There was a click; someone had hung up the phone in the kitchen. "Worse than yesterday," Kate said. "I didn't think that was possible. Cheer me up and tell me what's happening."

"Well, the skiing's been great so far. It's snowing now, so there's not any skiing tonight," Jody said. "That's okay, though, because Sasha already organized a party. There are two gigantic subs stuffed with ham and cheese and salami sitting in the kitchen right now. I think I could eat one of them by myself, I'm so hungry."

Jody heard herself babbling on and knew she was trying to keep Kate from asking about Leahna. "We had this contest on the trail before," she went on, watching Ellen towel her wet hair. "It was crazy, but nobody got hurt. Nobody fell, even. What we did was — "

"How are you getting along?" Kate broke in. "I mean, with all those strangers you were so worried about?"

"Fine."

"What do you think of Cal? Isn't he incredible? Drew's not bad, either, you notice."

"Yep."

"Chris'd die for him."

"Uh-huh."

"Oh," Kate said. "Somebody's in the room with you, am I right?"

"You got it." Ellen was pulling clothes out of her bag now, obviously trying not to listen. But Jody knew it was impossible. How could you not listen when the only person in the room with you was talking on the telephone? "Like I said," she added, "it's been great so far."

"Okay, I'll get to the point," Kate said. "Leahna. She showed up, didn't she?"

"Well, yes." Here it comes, Jody thought.

Kate let out her breath. "Well? Oh, right, you can't talk. Okay, did anything happen? Did she come on to Cal?"

"Not that I could see." That was being honest, at least. As far as Jody could tell, Leahna had acted kind of aloof.

"Never mind, she doesn't flirt," Kate said. "She just stands back and waits for guys to act like idiots around her, like she deserves their attention or something. Then she looks amused." She paused. "Did Cal? Fall all over her, I mean?"

"Uh, no, nobody fell."

"You know what I mean," Kate said sharply. "He did, didn't he? I knew he would. She's so great-looking, guys don't bother to find out what she's like. And by then it's too late. Is she coming to the party?"

"I don't know." Jody suddenly hated the way Kate sounded, so mean and vicious. Maybe Leahna was a beautiful creep, but there was nothing Kate could do about her. Or about Cal, either. "I really don't know," Jody said again. "Listen, I think I just heard a bunch of people come in downstairs. I guess the party's about ready to start."

"Okay. Let me say hi to Sasha, will you?" Kate said. "I'll talk to you again, tomorrow, maybe."

"Okay. I hope you get better fast." Jody lay the phone down quickly before Kate had a chance to say anything more. She went out to the railing over-looking the living room, and saw Sasha talking to some kids she didn't recognize. "Sasha?" Jody called. "Kate's on the phone, wants to say hi."

"Thanks, I'll get it in the kitchen."

Back in the bedroom, Jody waited until she heard Sasha's voice on the extension, then hung up and went over to the mirror hanging above a low, white chest of drawers. Her hair, dark-brown and naturally curly, was almost dry. She leaned close to the mirror and started putting on some eye shadow. Ellen was standing behind her, in the middle of the room, and their eyes met.

Ellen smiled. "I wish my hair would curl like that."

"It's murder in the summer," Jody said. "Curls so tight I have trouble getting a comb through it."

Ellen ran a comb through her own hair, which was fine and straight. "Jody? Could I ask you something?"

"Sure."

Ellen glanced at the door and bit her lip. Then she said, "Do you think I could ever have a chance with Cal?"

"*Cal?*" Jody almost dropped her makeup brush. "I thought you . . ."

"I know. You thought I was in love with Drew." Ellen smiled again. "Drew's a friend. I've known him a long time. I'm not comfortable with very many people, but I am with him."

Jody turned around and leaned against the chest. "Drew's . . . well, he doesn't seem like the most comfortable person to be with."

Ellen's laugh was as airy as her voice. "I know, it's funny, isn't it? His moods go up and down like a roller coaster. I guess I'm just used to them and they don't bother me." She looked down and picked a piece of fuzz off her navy sweater. "But it's Cal I love," she said in a low voice.

Jody cleared her throat. Talk about feeling uncomfortable. "Well, I don't really know Cal at all," she said. "Is he going out with anybody?"

Ellen shook her head. "He'd like to be going out with Leahna, anybody can see that."

"Well, but maybe he just likes the way she looks," Jody said. She knew it was more than that, but Ellen sounded so sad, she wanted to cheer her up. "I mean, she *is* beautiful."

"Sure. She's beautiful like Snow White's stepmother," Ellen said. "Inside she's rotten. I can't believe Cal doesn't see it."

"Chris told me about how she dropped Drew," Jody said. "It sounded pretty awful."

Ellen nodded. "She does things like that all the time. I don't mean just dropping boys, though. Once I thought she was my friend. She acted like one, anyway. We went to the library together and to the movies a couple of times, stuff like that." Ellen was staring into the distance, remembering. "She was in between boys at the time, so I should have guessed. But I didn't. She knew I'd been working on this essay for a statewide contest, and she offered to read it and make suggestions, you know. So naturally, I let her. And she stole it."

"What do you mean? You mean, she wrote the same thing?" Jody asked. "How come the teacher or judges or whatever didn't notice?"

"First we had to submit an idea to our English teacher," Ellen said. "The teacher told me my idea was good, but Leahna had had it first." Ellen's lips curled in a little smile. "She beat me to it. And her essay got into the finals."

"What did you say to her?"

"Nothing."

"Nothing?" Jody couldn't believe it. "Why didn't you tell the teacher? How come you let her get away with it?"

"Because I was afraid." Ellen blinked and shifted her gaze to Jody. "But she'll pay for it some day, you know. She'll pay for everything, I'm sure of it. I just hope it happens before she gets to Cal, because she'll hurt him, too. She takes and takes and never gives. She's rotten."

Ellen was talking softly, as usual, but there was ice in her voice. Jody shuddered a little.

"I'm sorry," Ellen said. "I shouldn't have said anything."

"It's okay. It's just that I can't tell you anything about Cal or what he's thinking. I don't know him," Jody said. "I don't really know you, either, or anybody else, hardly." She realized she sounded kind of cold. "Couldn't you ask Sasha about this?"

Ellen burst out laughing.

Jody looked at her curiously.

"Sorry, I'm not laughing at you, not really." Ellen took a deep breath. "Never mind, Jody. I should never have asked you. It wasn't fair, because you're right, you don't know any of us." She laughed again, almost a giggle, then stopped herself. "I think I'll go down and get something to eat before the food disappears. Thanks for listening to me, Jody."

When Ellen had gone, Jody leaned against the

chest and closed her eyes. First Chris, then Kate, then Ellen. One friend and two people she barely knew, and they were all obsessed with Leahna Calder. She shuddered, remembering the way they'd sounded, so full of bitterness. Her head was starting to ache — the last half hour had been a little too much.

A blast of music suddenly thundered up from below, and Jody fluffed up her hair and headed for the door. She was ready for a party. With dozens of people around, she could hide in the crowd and not get too close to *anybody*.

Chapter 4

The party *should* have been great. It started out exactly as Jody wanted. But by the end, she began to wish she'd never been a part of it.

At first it was fun. There were at least twenty people, not counting Jody's group, and she didn't know a single one. Nobody was being serious, either. Well, Drew had a frown on his face, but Jody decided that was normal for him half the time.

Jody enjoyed herself, just wandering around from group to group, listening but not talking much. It was almost impossible to talk, anyway, the music was so loud. But that was okay. She wasn't in the mood to talk.

Sasha was the center of the party, which didn't surprise Jody a bit. Dressed in sweatpants and a sweatshirt, with no makeup and her hair tied back with a piece of yarn, she still managed to look more beautiful than anyone. She danced a little and laughed a lot and was constantly on the move, her pale blue eyes searching out everyone, as if she wanted to make sure they were having fun.

Everyone was, at first. Well, Chris looked a little glum because Drew wasn't paying any attention to her; she prowled the edges of the room and always kept coming back to Drew, who was slouched in a low chair near the fire, watching the front door. Cal kept a hopeful eye on the door, too, Jody noticed. He was waiting for Leahna, she thought. She guessed Drew was, too, but he didn't look hopeful. He looked edgy, as if he wasn't sure whether he wanted her to come or not. But everybody else kept shouting at each other over the music, joking and swapping ski stories.

"Jody!" Billy called out when she walked into the kitchen. "Better hurry, the subs won't last forever."

Jody grabbed a wide wedge of one of the sandwiches and bit into it. She was famished.

"There's lots to drink," Billy told her, opening the refrigerator. "Coke, 7-Up, diet, regular, caffeine-free?"

"Later," Jody mumbled, her mouth full. People were milling around, brushing past her to get to the food. "I was wondering where you were," she said to Billy. "How come you're hanging out in here?"

"Sasha asked if I'd sort of take charge of the food, make sure we don't run out." Billy smiled, his mouth glistening with lip balm. "I guess my new image needs some more work. But hey, did you notice how I made that run today without crippling myself?"

"You did great." Jody didn't think Sasha had noticed, though. She'd been watching Leahna, like almost everyone else. "What happened, anyway? With Leahna, I mean?"

"I was just getting up the nerve to go down, and she came along," Billy said. "Kind of surprised me because nobody else was coming up on the lift by then. Anyway, we could hear you guys laughing, and she asked me what was going on, so I told her about the orange peel. So she goes, 'What's the prize if you get it?' And I said I didn't know if there was one, but Sasha would probably come up with something. She acted really excited when she found out it was Sasha and Cal down there. I was telling her about how Chris had knocked the orange peel out of reach, but she just laughed and said, 'Watch this.' Then she took off." Billy shook his head in wonder. "I couldn't believe it when she actually stabbed the thing."

"Nobody else could, either," Jody said. "Do you know her?"

"Not really. I've seen her around, though."

"I was just wondering if she's as bad as she sounds," Jody said. "I got an earful about her from Chris and Ellen."

"Well, I got the feeling Sasha isn't crazy about her, either," Billy said. "I heard her tell Drew the party wouldn't be ruined if she didn't show up."

"Listen," Jody said, "you shouldn't be staying in here all the time. People can find their own food. Why don't you go ask Sasha to dance or something?"

"I dance about as well as I ski," Billy said. He looked hopefully toward the living room. "But maybe I'll go talk to her."

After Billy left, Jody got herself a can of Coke and was just about ready to go back into the living room when Drew and Cal came into the kitchen. "Jody, how's it going, you having a good time?" Cal asked. Without waiting for an answer, he crossed to the telephone and started dialing. Jody looked at Drew, but he was watching Cal. Jody shrugged and left the room.

Over by the fireplace, Billy had edged close to Sasha and was gesturing wildly with his hands as he talked to her. Jody winced when one of his flying hands hit Sasha's cup, sending it halfway across the room where it landed with a splash at someone's feet.

Sasha laughed and patted him on the shoulder, then she leaned close and said something in his ear. Billy scurried off toward the kitchen, passing Jody on the way. "Did you see that trick?" he asked, his face redder than ever. "I've got a million of them."

"It could happen to anybody," Jody said.

"Yeah, but not on somebody's Navajo rug." Billy gulped a little. "Sasha said there's some kind of special cleaner in the kitchen. I hope it works." He turned and hurried on, almost bumping into Cal, who was on his way back in.

Jody spotted an empty chair near the fireplace and got to it fast. She sank down and closed her eyes a minute. The cold air and the skiing before, and now the heat of the room, were making her sleepy.

"You should see yourself, Cal," Jody heard Sasha say. "You keep watching the door like you're waiting for the Second Coming or something."

Jody kept her eyes closed.

"I'm not the only one," Cal said. "But Drew's not watching the door anymore. He just went over to her cabin."

"Fine, wonderful. That'll be one less person dragging the party down."

"Yeah, but what if he comes back with her?"

Sasha didn't answer, at least not directly. "I wish you could just forget her."

Cal was quiet for a minute. Then he said, "So do I, Sash. But things change."

He sounded so sad, Jody thought. She opened her eyes and looked around. That's when she saw Ellen standing nearby. Ellen had obviously overheard the conversation, too. She was staring into the distance the way she had earlier, but her jaw was clenched tightly, as if she were trying not to scream in anger.

"You're right, things do change." Sasha's voice was suddenly loud and excited. "And I think it's time for a change right now. Everybody!" she called out over the music. "Time for games, okay? Party games!"

Jody opened her eyes and saw Sasha striding toward the wall unit, where she shut off the CD player. She whirled around and faced everyone, her cheeks bright with color. "Enough standing around mindlessly stuffing yourselves, let's do something really fun!"

"I'm having fun already," someone quipped.

"Maybe, but look at Billy." Sasha pointed to Billy, down on his knees with a sponge, rubbing at the rug. "He can't possibly be enjoying himself. Billy, I'm sure you've got it, if you keep going, you'll rub a hole in the rug." She laughed and pointed to a chair in the center of the room. "Go sit there, okay, and we'll start the game."

Still holding the sponge, Billy took the chair. Sasha rummaged around in a drawer of the wall unit and came up with her hands full of pencils and small pads of paper.

"Pictionary?" someone asked. "I hate that game."

"That's okay, we're not playing it." Sasha looked at Cal, and they smiled at each other. Whatever was wrong between them seemed to have been forgotten. "This is much better."

"So what is it?" Chris asked.

"Truth," Cal said.

Someone groaned, but Cal ignored it. "One person sits in the chair and the rest of us write something down about him. Somebody reads the statements, and the person has to say whether they're true or not."

This time it was Jody who groaned, but she did it silently. She'd played this game before, or at least a version of it, and it always got embarrassing. Just because it was a game, people seemed to think it was okay to dredge up all kinds of secrets. You could lie, of course, but half the time your face gave you away. And whoever'd written the secret would call you on it.

Looking around the room, Jody saw that there weren't as many people as there had been earlier. She guessed some of them had gone on to other parties, or maybe to the lodge, or just to bed. She was tempted to go upstairs to bed herself, but she didn't want to get caught trying to sneak out of this. She sank down farther into the chair.

Sasha went around the room, passing out pencils and paper. When she was finished, she went over and stood next to Billy. "This is Billy Feldman," she said. "He's sixteen, and if you don't know him, then just take a guess at something."

Billy watched as people started scribbling on their pads. He looked like he was on trial.

"Remember," Sasha said, "you can't write easy stuff like 'You'd like to be rich.' This game is supposed to force people to be honest, even if it's embarrassing. And there's nothing embarrassing about wanting money."

Jody thought a minute, then wrote, *You sometimes wish you were somebody else.* From what she knew of Billy, it had to be true. And it wasn't prying, either. Lots of people wished that.

After a moment, Cal gathered the slips of paper from everyone. "Ready?" he asked Billy.

"Aren't I supposed to get a hearty meal first?" Billy said. "No, I already had one. Actually I had three. Okay, okay, go ahead. Let me have it. How bad can it be?"

The first statement was *You never lie.*

"Obviously, somebody took a guess," Billy said, looking relieved. "Not true. I do lie. I admit it."

Cal read the next statement. It was Jody's. Billy listened, then shook his head. "Not true." He grinned. "I *always* wish I were someone else."

"Go on, Cal," Sasha urged.

"If you didn't laugh at yourself, you'd be the only one not laughing," Cal read.

Somebody whistled. Jody looked at Chris, wondering if she'd written it. Chris was picking at a fingernail, looking bored.

"I knew something like this was coming," Billy said. He squeezed the sponge, dripping water on his jeans. "Well. How do I know? I mean, I can't speak for everybody. I can't answer it."

"But you have to," Sasha said softly. She was sitting on the rug, her long legs curled under her.

"Okay, true," Billy said quickly. He was starting to look trapped. His soft brown eyes darted around the room as if he were looking for a way to escape. "Next question, please."

Cal looked at the next slip of paper. "Um . . . it says, *You hate Sasha.*"

Sasha's eyes widened, but she looked eager to hear the answer.

Billy leaned over until his forehead was touching his knees. His shoulders shook a little, and Jody thought he must be laughing. It was a ridiculous question, she thought. Anyone with eyes could see that Billy was wild about Sasha.

"Billy?" Cal said.

Billy slowly raised his head. His eyes were bright, but not with laughter. He glanced around the room again and stopped when he saw Jody. He looked straight at her. "I thought we could be friends," he said, his voice pleading.

Jody felt like someone had punched her in the stomach.

No one else seemed to have noticed that Billy was speaking directly to Jody.

"Does that mean it's not true?" Cal asked.

"What?" Billy blinked. Finally he looked away from Jody. "Oh. Yes. Not true."

"Well, that's a relief," Sasha said, with a light laugh. "Of course we can be friends, Billy. We *are* friends."

"Great." Billy stood up, the sponge still gripped in his hand.

"Hey, where are you going?" Cal jabbed him playfully on the shoulder. "Your time's not up yet, buddy."

Billy started to say something, but before he could, the front door opened and Drew came in, a gust of cold wind blowing behind him. He was alone.

"Drew!" Sasha said, leaping to her feet. "You're just in time. We're playing Truth. You can join us."

Drew didn't answer at first. He was stomping snow off his boots, his head down. When he looked up, he and Cal exchanged glances. Drew's face was dark with anger. Cal's shoulders sagged, and the hopeful expression disappeared from his face.

"Hey, what's it like out there now?" someone asked Drew. "Still snowing?"

"I didn't notice," Drew said shortly. As he shrugged out of his jacket, several kids went to the front window, cupping their hands against the glass so they could see outside, talking about what the slopes would be like tomorrow.

But Jody didn't join in. Billy had taken advantage of the break to slip out of the room and go into the kitchen, and Jody decided to follow him. She had to straighten things out.

On her way through the living room, she got stuck for a moment behind Cal, who had moved over next to Drew.

"Is she leaving tomorrow?" Cal was asking Drew.

"You think she'd be straight and tell me?" Drew said. "She laughed and said she wasn't sure. Like you can just pick up and fly from Brevard to Antigua without having to plan ahead."

Jody put her hand lightly on Cal's back, thinking he'd step aside, but he didn't seem to notice.

"Maybe I'll go over, talk to her," Cal said. "You don't mind, I mean . . ."

"Hey, I'm through, she's all yours, buddy," Drew said bitterly.

"Come on, Drew," Chris said, brushing past Jody and slipping her arm through Drew's. "There's an empty chair by the fireplace. Come sit down."

Drew glanced at her, then back at Cal. "Go if you want to," he said. "But if you want my advice, don't waste your time."

"Come on, Drew!" Chris gave his arm an impatient tug, and finally the three of them shifted, and Jody was able to get by.

"Jody, if you see Billy, would you bring him back?" Sasha called out to her. "We're going to get started again."

"I'll tell him, but I have the feeling he doesn't want to sit in the hot seat anymore."

"No?" Sasha looked surprised. "Why?"

Jody stared at her. Had she really missed the trapped look on Billy's face? "I just don't think he was having any fun, that's all."

"Oh, sure he was. Everybody knows it's just a game. Nobody takes it seriously." Sasha smiled and spun back toward the rest of the group.

Maybe she's right, Jody thought, heading on to the kitchen. Maybe Billy hadn't really been looking at Jody when he'd said he thought they were friends. Nobody else had picked up on it, so maybe she'd just imagined the whole thing.

The kitchen was empty, except for Billy. He was standing at the sink, splashing water on his face.

"Billy?" Jody said.

He held up a hand, gesturing for her to wait. Then he reached for the paper towel holder, which spun out of control, sending about twenty of the towels into a pile on the counter. Billy fumbled at them, tore off too many, and blotted his face. His back was still to Jody.

Finally, he turned around, crumpling the towels into a ball in his fist. "How did you know?" he asked quietly. "Until tonight, I didn't even realize that I hate Sasha. So how did you figure it out?"

Chapter 5

Jody felt as if the wind had been knocked out of her again. Coming from Billy, the word *hate* sounded foreign. He was too soft, too puppy-doggish for such a strong word. But there he was, his jaw tight, his eyes hard. He didn't look soft at all. He looked perfectly capable of hating, maybe even hating Jody herself.

"You look surprised," Billy said. "Actually, you look shocked. Why?"

Jody felt behind her for one of the kitchen chairs, swung it around to face him and sat down. "I came in here to tell you that I didn't write that — about hating Sasha," she said. "I never expected you to say you do."

Billy leaned his head back and stared at the ceiling. "Me and my big mouth," he said, his chin still in the air. "I should have let you talk first. Then I could have laughed the whole thing off."

"Jody, Billy!" Ellen's voice was calling from the living room. "Everybody's ready to play again."

Jody turned sideways and shouted, "I dropped

45

the potato salad, and we're cleaning it up. Go ahead, start without us!" When she turned back, Billy was grinning at her.

"You lie, too," he said.

"Sometimes, but I'm not lying about what I wrote," Jody said. "I wrote the one about wishing you were somebody else."

"Well, like I said, I thought you'd guessed the truth about Sasha. I don't know why, maybe it's because you listen and watch a lot," he said.

There was laughter from the living room, and they heard Ellen saying, "Oh, no, do I have to answer?" She giggled, and Jody could almost see her blushing.

"Hey, why don't you go back in?" Billy said, tossing the wad of paper towels into the wastebasket. "I can tell you're embarrassed to be with me, now that you know my big secret."

"I'm not embarrassed," Jody told him. "I'm shocked. I thought you were crazy about Sasha."

"Me, too. It's wild, isn't it?" Billy said. "I think it was the rug."

"The rug?"

"Yeah, when I was cleaning it up, it just kind of hit me — there I was, down on my knees, scrubbing away so she wouldn't be mad. So she'd thank me, notice me, whatever. Then I realized it couldn't be a *real* Navajo rug. If it were, it would probably be on the wall, not the floor. But she let me believe it was priceless." He shrugged. "I usually hate myself when I get into a situation like that, but this time I hated *her*. For making me feel like a nerd."

Billy turned back to the sink and stared out of the window above it. "Leahna," he said.

"What?"

"That's Leahna's cabin, right across from us," Billy said. "I saw her through the window just before you came in. She's not there now." He turned around. "She's like Sasha, I've decided. The way she talked to me up on the slope today, like I was invisible. They're two of a kind, and I hate them both."

"Billy . . ."

"Hey, don't look at me like that," he said. "*I'm* not the one who treats people like dirt."

There was another burst of laughter from the living room.

"Go on, Jody," Billy said, turning his back on her again. "Just go on."

Shaken by the anger in his voice, Jody got up and left the room. Sasha was coming toward the kitchen and immediately asked about Billy.

"He's . . . I think he's tired," Jody said, moving farther into the living room, away from the kitchen.

"No, I've been thinking about what you said, and he *was* upset, wasn't he?" Sasha asked. "I wish I knew who wrote that, about how if he didn't laugh at himself, he'd be the only one. It wasn't very nice."

"No," Jody agreed. She started to say what he was *really* upset about, but then she changed her mind. Here was Sasha, looking worried and sorry that Billy might be upset. Was that the kind of person who treated people like dirt? Maybe Billy had her all wrong. Jody didn't know and suddenly

47

didn't want to think about it anymore.

"Well, maybe we should just leave him alone," Sasha said. "Come on, let's see how Ellen's holding up."

Jody was hardly excited about more Truth, but she let herself be pulled back into the living room. The crowd had gotten smaller now. There were only three or four kids left who weren't actually staying at the cabin.

Ellen was in the hot seat, tugging at a strand of her light-brown hair. "I hope I'm almost finished," she said shyly to Cal. "I don't think I can stand much more." Actually she looked pretty happy, Jody thought, probably because Cal was standing so close to her.

"Three more to go, then you're free," Cal told her, glancing at his watch. He looked down at the next paper and read, "*You're in love with Drew.*"

Drew snorted.

"Hey, wait," Cal said, "the next one says you're in love with me!"

Sasha laughed. "Maybe she loves both of you."

"Give her a break," Drew said.

Chris looked at him sharply, but she kept her voice light. "No, she has to answer."

Ellen's face was bright red, and she covered it with her hands. "Not true," she said.

"Which one?" Sasha laughed.

"Not true," Ellen said again, her voice muffled by her fingers.

"Does that mean both?" Chris asked.

"Let's say it does and get this over with." Cal

flipped to the last piece of paper, started to read, and then stopped. "This isn't funny," he said quietly.

"None of it's been that funny," Drew commented.

"Go on, Cal," Sasha said. "You're the one in a hurry. Read it."

Cal crumpled the paper and let it drop, but Chris snatched it up. "I'll do it," she said, smoothing it out. Her eyes widened, and she gave a short laugh. "Are you ready for this? It says *You wish Leahna Calder were dead*."

Ellen lowered her hands and stood up. Her face was white now. "But that's . . ." She gave her head a shake. "That's enough."

Jody thought Ellen would go upstairs, but instead she took her jacket and walked out the door. Jody wondered who'd written that one. Whoever it was must know Ellen pretty well. Except Ellen didn't really want Leahna *dead*. She just wanted her punished, maybe, or paid back.

The three people who weren't staying at the cabin stood up. "Listen, I think we'll be going," one of them said. "See everybody tomorrow, probably."

When the door shut behind them, everyone was quiet for a minute. Then Sasha said, "I feel awful." She looked disappointed. "And this was going to be such a great party."

"Can't win 'em all, Sash." Cal was rummaging through the puffy down jackets by the door. He dug his out and pulled it on.

"You're going out?" Sasha asked. "Cal, I — "

"I know." He zipped up his parka and smiled at

her, his eyes bright. "Cheer up, Sasha. Maybe I won't be long." He left, slamming the door behind him. Jody wished he were going after Ellen, but she was pretty sure he was heading for Leahna's place.

Sasha stared at the closed door for a second, then she swung around, moving gracefully from table to table. "Time to clean up. I'm sorry the party turned out this way," she said, her long fingers quickly gathering up empty cups and stacking them together. "Maybe we'll have another one tomorrow night. A better one. I'll talk to Cal about it. Or maybe somebody else will have one. There's always a party going on around here." Her cheerful voice trailed off as she went into the kitchen.

Jody decided not to volunteer for kitchen duty. She'd had enough — of everything — for one night and she was suddenly so tired she wasn't sure she could make it up the stairs.

The girls' bedroom was dark, and Jody left it that way while she got undressed and into a pair of light-weight sweatpants and a soft T-shirt. Switching on a light, she gathered up her toothbrush and toothpaste, then went down to the small half-bathroom at the end of the hall. The guys' half of the top floor was dark, too, and she wondered if Billy was in there, asleep. She brushed her teeth and walked back, her legs feeling like lead.

Jody turned off the light, unfolded a heavy blanket, and crawled into bed, spreading the blanket out on top of her. Her bed was under the eave; if she turned toward the wall, her head would hit the sloping ceiling. She rolled over onto her stomach, sure that she'd be asleep in a few seconds.

But as soon as she closed her eyes, images started flashing through her mind: Billy hanging over the van seat, eagerly talking to Sasha. Chris looking daggers at her because of Drew. Ellen's white face when she left the living room. Drew, stomping angrily into the cabin after going to Leahna's. Sasha and Cal, their identical blue eyes sending messages to each other. And Billy again, licking his chapped lips, scrubbing at the rug, and later in the kitchen, his eyes dark with hatred.

Downstairs, a door slammed. Jody opened her eyes and listened, expecting to hear footsteps on the stairs. But the cabin stayed quiet. She rolled onto her back and closed her eyes again, but this time, her thoughts kept her awake. The game of Truth should be banned, she decided. Too many ugly feelings came out when you played it. If there was really so much hate around, it should be kept hidden. People had bad thoughts about other people all the time, but they were private, not party material.

The door to the bedroom swung open, and Jody sat up, bumping her head on the ceiling. "Who is it?" she asked, rubbing her head.

"Chris."

In the light from the hallway, Jody saw Chris move like a shadow toward her own bed. "You going to sleep?" Jody asked.

"Not yet. It's not even midnight." There was some shuffling, and Chris clicked her tongue impatiently. "Where are they?"

"What?"

"My gloves . . . oh, there they are."

Jody blinked. "You're going out?"

"Why not? It stopped snowing. Everybody else did."

"Everybody?"

"I don't really know, it seems like it." Chris sounded in a hurry; she was moving back toward the door now. "This place is dead. I'm walking down to the lodge — maybe there's some action there." She went out, shutting the door behind her, leaving Jody in the dark.

Jody lay back down, carefully avoiding the ceiling. Maybe she'd just imagined all those hateful feelings swirling around the cabin like smoke. Maybe everyone had laughed it all off and they were down at the lodge having fun, while she was up here, knocking her head against the ceiling. It would serve her right for taking everything so seriously.

For a second, Jody considered going to the lodge, too. But she'd warmed up the bed already, and she was feeling too lazy to get dressed and pull on boots and stuff. Besides, she wasn't even sure where the lodge was.

She felt lazy, but she was also wide awake now. Rolling over, she propped her chin in her hands and looked out the window. Chris was right: It had stopped snowing.

The view into Leahna Calder's cabin window was crystal-clear.

The Lovely Leahna, Jody thought. And just as she thought it, there Leahna was, moving across the room. It looked like she was getting ready to go out. Jody's eyes widened, then squinted, so she could see better. She scooted up a little until her forehead was pressed against the cold glass.

Suddenly Leahna turned her head and looked off, toward the door, Jody guessed. Then she walked out of the room.

Jody's eyes drifted away, toward the other cabins and the snow-covered paths between them. She could see a few people walking, slipping along like dark ghosts. She could even see the frosty puffs of their breath in the cold air.

A movement caught Jody's eye, and she jerked her head toward Leahna's window again. Leahna was back, but not alone. Someone was with her.

Jody pushed her head closer to the window, mashing the tip of her nose. Leahna's visitor hadn't come far enough into the room for Jody to see much. Even so, she could tell that this was not a friendly visit.

Leahna shook her head. Her visitor jabbed the air with a finger. Jody saw something flash, a chain, maybe, or a watch. Leahna took a few steps back, then shook her head again.

Jody's breath had completely fogged up the glass. She wiped it away and covered her nose.

Leahna had tossed her head back; was she laughing? She pointed toward the door, maybe telling the visitor to go. The visitor didn't move.

As Jody wiped the glass again, Leahna strode toward her visitor, making a shooing motion with her hands. The visitor's arms shot out, and suddenly Leahna was stumbling backward, tripping and falling onto the floor.

The visitor stood still for a moment, then turned and disappeared from view.

Leahna was out of Jody's view, too. But then Leahna was standing up again, her eyes on the spot where the visitor had been. She rubbed a shoulder, ran her fingers through her hair, and shrugged.

Then she came to the window and cupped her hands against it, almost mirroring Jody.

Jody immediately ducked down, then laughed at herself. She was in the dark and couldn't be seen. She popped her head back up.

Leahna's window was empty.

Jody felt almost disappointed. She had no idea who Leahna's visitor was or what they were arguing about, but it had been an exciting little drama and it was over too fast. Too bad she hadn't been able to hear them, or at least read their lips.

Suddenly Jody tensed. Was that somebody coming up the stairs? She listened closely, but the cabin stayed quiet. Nobody came.

Jody let her breath fog the window again and then wrote her name in it. She suddenly felt ashamed of herself, playing the peeping Tom, safe in the dark, looking at two people who had no idea they were being watched. She'd had no right to do that. She sure wouldn't want anybody watching *her*.

With a sigh, Jody put her head down and pulled the blanket up over her shoulders. Billy had said she listened and watched a lot. She'd never realized it, but maybe he was right. She sure had done enough of it tonight, and look what had happened. She'd seen people crying and arguing, heard them saying ugly things they probably didn't mean. Tomorrow, she decided, she'd keep her ears closed and her eyes on the snowy slopes of Brevard Pass.

But even as Jody drifted off to sleep, the scene in Leahna's window flashed through her mind. She saw the visitor's arms reach out and shove Leahna away, hard enough to make her fall.

Jody shivered a little. It hadn't really been an exciting drama. It was actually kind of scary, knowing that somebody was mad enough to do that.

Leahna should be careful, Jody thought. She has a lot of enemies.

Chapter 6

Bright sunshine woke Jody up, streaming through the big glass window onto her face. She turned over and looked out, and the first things she saw were her name streaked across the window and the big smudge on the glass where she'd kept wiping the fog away. The memory of last night came flooding back, and she moved over and tried to see into Leahna's window. But the glare of the sun made it impossible, and she felt disappointed. Maybe she'd uncovered a dark secret about herself — Jody Sanderson, window spy.

Hearing soft, even breathing in the room, Jody sat on the edge of the bed and looked around. At the other end of the room, Chris was almost buried under her blanket, one spike of bright blonde hair sticking out. On the bed next to hers, Ellen was curled on her side, clutching the pillow in both hands. Sasha's bed was empty.

Not wanting to wake anyone, Jody quietly eased out of bed. The room was cold, and she shivered as she pulled on a sweatshirt. She went out and brushed her teeth, then headed for the stairs, smelling coffee the closer she got to the kitchen.

"Hi, Jody." Sasha greeted her from the kitchen table, where she sat with her hands around a cup of coffee. She looked tired, with shadowy circles under her eyes. "I'm glad somebody else is up. I hate sitting alone."

There was a box of blueberry muffins on the counter. Jody took one and poured herself some coffee. "I'm surprised anybody's up but me," she said, pulling out a chair and sitting down. "When I went to sleep last night, I was still the only one in the room." She wolfed down half a muffin. "Chris said she was going to the lodge. Is that where everybody else went? Did I miss anything great?"

"I don't know, I didn't go there," Sasha said. "I went to some friends' cabin. But there's always something going on at the lodge, so if you missed anything last night, you can try it tonight." She got up and spilled the last of her coffee into the sink.

"It's too early to think about tonight," Jody said. "All I can think about now is getting down the slopes. It's going to be a great day."

"Yes. I hope so." Sasha picked up a towel draped over one of the chairs and went to the door. "Time for a shower. See you later, Jody."

A couple of minutes after Sasha left, Drew came in, followed by Billy. Then Ellen came downstairs, and then Cal and Chris, and the kitchen was full of hungry people. Jody'd told herself last night that she wasn't going to do so much watching and listening. But she couldn't help trying to get a sense of their moods, to see if there were any bad feelings left over from the party.

It was hard to tell. Ellen and Drew were quiet. In fact, no one talked much at all. Chris looked a little grumpy, but that was her usual expression. Billy yawned most of the time and avoided looking at Jody. Cal didn't say a word, and Jody wondered if he'd gone to see Leahna last night.

Maybe he had. Maybe he was the one she'd seen in the window.

The house had warmed up by now, but the mood in the kitchen was cold and unfriendly. For a while, the day before, Jody had felt like she was getting to know these people and to like some of them. Now she felt as if she were in a room full of strangers again.

But it was morning, she told herself. Everybody had just gotten up and they were barely awake. Maybe she was exaggerating things.

Of course, she hadn't exaggerated the argument she'd seen between Leahna and her visitor. That had been ugly and *real*. And the harder Jody tried to forget it, the more she thought about it.

The snow had added an inch of powder, but the night had been cold, and the slopes were icy and incredibly fast. The sun didn't help much; it was still so cold the snow squeaked. It was too fast for Jody; she fell three times during a single run. As she picked herself up from the last fall, she decided to get something to eat. Food might not help her ski any better, but at least it would cheer her up.

Rather than go back to the cabin, Jody decided to check out the lodge. It was a big wood-and-stone building with tall windows, and she figured she'd sit and watch everyone else skiing while she got warm and full.

The dining room was enormous, with a big stone fireplace blazing away, and it was crowded. All the window tables were taken, and most of the others were, too. Jody was looking for someplace to sit when she heard her name called.

"Jody, over here." It was Drew, sitting at a window table with Chris, waving for her to join them.

Jody waved back and started threading her way through people and tables. Chris probably wasn't thrilled to have her sit with them, but Jody was too hungry to care.

"Thanks," Jody said when she got to them. "I was beginning to think I'd have to eat standing up."

Drew pushed a chair out with his foot, and Jody sat down and looked around.

"This place is huge," she said. "Big enough for a band and stuff." She looked at Chris. "Was there one last night?"

"You were here last night?" Drew said to Chris.

"I was, for a while, but I didn't see you."

"Too bad," Chris murmured. "I guess we were here at different times." She frowned at her menu.

Jody picked up her own menu. If Chris wanted to ignore her, fine. Jody could ignore with the best of them. "What's good to eat here?" She asked Drew.

"Stick with the hamburgers," he advised.

"Everything else is too expensive and not that great."

Jody ordered a cheeseburger, and because she was still cold, some cream-of-mushroom soup. When the soup came, she tasted it and wished she hadn't. She reached for her water and caught Drew looking at her. One eyebrow was raised. "Okay, okay," she laughed. "You told me so."

"I didn't say a word," he protested.

"You didn't have to. I knew you were dying to."

"True," he admitted. "Are you always that good at figuring out what people are thinking?"

"It didn't take much to figure that out." Jody snuck a look at Chris. It didn't take much to figure out what *she* was thinking, either. She was wishing Jody would conveniently disappear.

In spite of Chris, Jody was enjoying herself. Drew in one of his good moods was very nice to be with.

Unfortunately, his good mood lasted about as long as his hamburger, which he demolished before Jody was even a third of the way through hers. Drew was teasing Jody, daring her to try the slope known as the Killer, when Chris, who'd been picking at a grilled cheese sandwich, suddenly laughed out loud. It was a short, sharp, bark of a laugh.

"What is it?" Drew asked.

"Nothing. I just saw something." Chris tore a strip of crust off her sandwich and nibbled on it, smirking a little. "I thought it was funny."

"Well?" Drew sounded impatient.

"Look." Chris pointed out the window to where a skier was trying to pick herself up after a fall. Jody wasn't surprised that Chris got a kick out of something like that — she probably laughed at old ladies falling down, too — but it was the kind of thing she thought even Chris would keep to herself. Then she saw who the skier was: Leahna Calder, dressed today in blue and neon-green, with a wide chartreuse headband holding back her long hair.

"She was almost at the bottom when she fell," Chris said. "She's probably wishing she did go to Antigua today. Look! Billy's helping her up."

Sure enough, Billy Feldman had come to Leahna's aid, standing pigeon-toed again, holding out his hand. Jody didn't understand why he bothered, after what he'd said the night before. Leahna waved him away and got to her feet alone.

Jody started to feel sorry for Billy, and then told herself to stop. She could only see what was happening, she couldn't hear. Leahna might have thanked him and said it was easier to get up by herself.

"Well!" Chris said, cheerfully polishing off another piece of crust, "I'm ready for some hot chocolate. What about you, Drew?"

But Drew just shook his head, his teasing, light-hearted mood gone. "I think it's time to get back on the slopes," he said grimly. He pushed his chair back and stood up, dropping a dollar bill on the table for a tip. Then he nodded at the two girls and left. Chris was on her feet before he was halfway across the dining room, hurrying after him. She didn't bother to say good-bye to Jody. She didn't add to the tip, either.

Sighing, Jody picked up her cheeseburger and bit into it, looking out the window. Billy had disappeared, but Leahna was still there. Cal was with her now, and the two of them were talking. Jody wondered again if Cal had gone to see her last night, like he'd said he was going to. Could he have been the visitor she'd seen through Leahna's window?

Jody dropped her burger into her plate, narrowing her eyes to get a better look, to see if she could tell whether their conversation was friendly. Leahna's visitor had shoved her backwards, made her fall. Would Cal do something like that? If he had, they'd hardly be talking to each other now, would they? Unless Cal was apologizing. Maybe . . .

Jody suddenly realized she was doing it again — watching through windows. She really ought to learn to mind her own business. She forced her eyes back to the table and deliberately thought about something else. Like whether or not she should add two dollars to the tip — one for herself and one for Chris. Or whether she should just add a single and let the waiter think she was the cheap one.

Jody had compromised on the tip — a dollar-fifty — and by the time she was outside again and riding up in the lift, everyone from the cabin was out of sight. Not out of mind, though, not completely. Jody couldn't help being curious about all the little dramas that seemed to be going on around her. But she'd compromised on that, too — as long as she just thought about them, but didn't say anything, then she wasn't being nosy.

Midway through the ride, the man next to her on the lift said, "Is it my imagination or has it gotten colder?"

"It's getting cloudy, so you're probably right," Jody said.

"Good. The skiing's going to get fast."

"It already is." Jody peered down, wondering if she'd made a mistake coming up again. She'd already fallen because of ice, and if it was getting worse, she'd definitely fall again. Well, she didn't have much choice. She could ride the lift down, of course. But nobody did that unless they broke a binding or something. Jody'd never been much of a risk-taker, but she wasn't ready to face total humiliation by riding an empty down-lift, either.

Once she got off the lift, she asked a couple of people about ice and they said some places were flagged, but it really wasn't any worse than it had been before.

They were wrong.

As soon as she pushed off, Jody knew this wasn't going to be an easy run. Twice she almost lost control, and when she came to a flat stretch, she stopped and got off the trail, into the powdery snow that hadn't been tamped down and hardened into what felt like a skating rink. She watched another skier whiz by, then took a deep breath and pushed off again.

The patch of ice took her by surprise, and as soon as Jody hit it, she knew it was all over. Her left ski shot out from under her, and she felt her body lifting into the air. She got rid of the poles and told herself to relax, go with the fall. But the edge of her right ski caught on something — ice, dirt, a root, she didn't know — and her right leg was dragging, going the wrong way. It finally joined the rest of her, but not before Jody felt a sharp pain in her ankle, a pain that shot halfway up her leg and made her cry out even before she'd hit the ground.

The landing knocked the breath out of her, and she was dizzy. She lay sprawled in the snow, black spots dancing behind her closed eyelids. She couldn't remember hitting her head, but she must have. Afraid to lose consciousness, she opened her eyes. The tops of the pine trees spun sickeningly in the bright blue sky, and a wave of nausea hit her. She closed her eyes and panted, frightened and hurt.

The next thing she felt was a hand on her arm. "Don't move," a voice said.

"No, the only thing I hurt is my ankle, and maybe my head," Jody said. She hadn't even heard the skier arrive — she must have blacked out for a second — but she leaned gratefully on the skier's arm and pushed herself to a sitting position. "I might be sick," she warned.

But she wasn't. Her stomach churned ominously for a few seconds, then settled down. Jody took a chance and opened her eyes. The first thing she saw were blue-covered legs with patches of neon-green on them. Then she looked up, into a lovely face framed by thick, taffy-colored hair pushed back with a chartreuse headband.

Leahna Calder. Everybody's enemy was now Jody's hero.

Leahna helped her get semi-comfortable, leaning against a tree trunk, then she said, "I'll go down and get the patrol." Her voice was matter-of-fact, as if she did this kind of thing all the time.

Jody watched as Leahna found her skis and poles and put them next to her, near the tree. She felt safe now, sore and cold, but safe.

Another skier came down the slope then, swooshed to a stop, and raised her goggles. "Jody!" Sasha cried. "Are you hurt bad?"

"I don't think so," Jody said. "My right ankle got it, but I think everything else is in one piece." She suddenly realized she hadn't even thanked Leahna for helping her, but it was too late, now. Leahna was already pushing off down the slope in a flash of blue and green, her long hair whipping out behind her. And then she was gone.

Chapter 7

Jody's ankle was sprained, not broken. A doctor at the lodge wrapped it up and then suggested she stay at the lodge overnight so the medical team could keep an eye on her.

"I don't understand," Jody said, leaning on Sasha for support as she got off the examining table. "Even if my ankle were broken . . ."

"Not your ankle," the doctor said. "Your head. There's no evidence of concussion but that doesn't always rule it out. You should be watched for twenty-four hours, just in case."

Jody was worn out. "Watched for what?" she asked tiredly.

"Dizziness, blurred vision, tingling in your fingers or toes, vomiting, unconsciousness." He reeled them off like a chant.

"She's staying with six other people," Sasha told him. "We'll check on her all the time, and if anything looks funny, we'll get her over here right away. That'll be all right, won't it?"

Sasha sounded responsible and competent, and

the doctor gave them both his blessing to go back to the cabin.

"I feel ridiculous," Jody said as she hobbled out of the room, leaning heavily on Sasha. "I knew the slopes were icy; I should never have gone back up." If she'd been in the mood, she might have laughed at herself: They hadn't had to take her down on a stretcher — she'd ridden the empty lift down, the humiliating ride she'd thought about taking on the way up.

"Don't be silly," Sasha said. "They weren't any worse than they were this morning. You didn't do anything stupid. It was just bad luck."

"I guess I should go back home," Jody said glumly. "I mean, I can't ski, so what's the point of staying? But my parents are away." Since she was taking a vacation, they'd decided to take one, too, and had flown to Arizona to visit some friends.

"Well, you shouldn't go tonight, anyway," Sasha said. "You should lie down and relax and then see how you feel tomorrow."

Jody didn't argue. Sasha was right — she had to stay overnight, at least. She couldn't go back to an empty house the way she felt right now. And what if she got worse on the bus or something? Still, she wanted to go home in the worst way. She was shivering and her ankle throbbed and her head ached. She wanted to be in her own bed, not in a strange bed, in a strange cabin, being watched over by people she hardly knew.

By the time Jody *was* in bed, though, she stopped feeling so sorry for herself. The rest of her group came back soon after she and Sasha did, and they all went out of their way to make her comfortable, offering to bring her magazines and hot chocolate and food. Even Chris didn't make any nasty remarks, which for her, *was* going out of her way, Jody figured, and probably took a supreme effort. Jody was grateful for all their attention and felt a little less lonely and homesick.

"So," Drew said, dropping a pile of magazines on her bed, "you had to do it, didn't you?"

"Do what?"

He grinned. "You mean you weren't on the Killer run?"

"Very funny, you know I wasn't." Jody picked up one of the magazines. "*Popular Mechanic*?"

"Hey, it was in the cabin. For all I know you could be a whiz in the garage." He chuckled and headed for the door. "Actually, I'll be glad to get you something else. I'm going out in a little while."

"No, that's okay, thanks." Jody was rifling through the pile of magazines. "There's other stuff here, and Sasha brought me some books." She scooted farther up on her pillow and winced.

Drew noticed. "I could get you some aspirin. You look like you could use it."

"Thanks, but I have aspirin. And the doctor gave me those." Jody pointed to a brown bottle on a low stool by the bed. "Pain pills. I'll take one later if I can't sleep."

"Looks like I'm useless," Drew said. "I'll stop by later, anyway, okay?"

"Sure." Jody smiled at him, hoping he would.

Ellen and Cal came in just as Drew was leaving. "She's not rational," Drew told them with a straight face. "I'm afraid it's just a matter of time." He shook his head sadly and went out the door.

"I don't know, you seem okay to me." Cal walked closer and peered at her. "Of course, your eyes are crossed, and you've got this huge point coming up out of your head, but that doesn't mean your mind is going."

"What do I have to do to get a little sympathy around here?" Jody laughed, and so did Cal, a little too hard. Even though he was joking, his voice sounded strained, and his eyes didn't light up when he smiled.

Ellen gazed at Cal. "You're terrible," she said to him. "Poor Jody's got enough to worry about."

"You're right," Cal agreed. He laughed again, sounding forced. "The point isn't that big."

"Cal!" Ellen covered her mouth and giggled. "Anyway, Jody, do you need anything else? Before dinner, I mean?"

"I'm fine, really," Jody said.

"How'd it happen?" Cal asked as they both sat on the floor next to the bed. "Give us the gory details. That's what we really came for."

"I just lost control on some ice," Jody said. "My right leg went one way and the rest of me went the other. I don't even remember hitting my head. Leahna told me not to move, but I was pretty sure nothing was broken, except maybe my ankle."

There was a silence. Jody looked at them and realized neither one of them knew Leahna had been there. Cal's face had tightened, closed up, and his light-blue eyes seemed darker. Jody wished she could read his mind. Was he still crazy about Leahna, or had he come to hate her, too?

Ellen was watching Cal with a smile that looked painted on. When she finally spoke, her voice was hard and brittle, the way it was when she'd talked about the essay. "Leahna? I thought Sasha found you."

"No, Leahna was the one." Jody felt uncomfortable, but she went on. "Then Sasha came and Leahna went down for help." She spread her hands and shrugged, laughing a little to fill up the silence. "That's it, the whole gruesome story."

Cal had been staring up at the window, frowning. Now he got to his feet, lithe and graceful, like his sister. "Well, I'm going to head down and see what's for dinner," he said. "Glad you're okay, Jody."

Ellen stayed where she was, picking at the rug with thin fingers. "So it was Leahna to the rescue," she said with a twisted smile.

Jody shifted in the bed, the bitterness in Ellen's voice making her uneasy. "Maybe she'll go to Antigua tonight or tomorrow."

"Maybe." Ellen's mouth twisted again.

Without thinking, Jody said, "I didn't thank her."

"Who. Sasha?"

Jody shook her head.

"Oh. Leahna." Ellen got up and looked out the window. "Well, you'd better do it soon, Jody, before it's too late." Without looking at Jody again, she turned and left the room.

Jody blew out her breath and leaned back against the pillows. What had Ellen meant by not waiting until it was too late? Did she mean before Leahna left for Antigua? That was the obvious answer, but that wasn't the way it had sounded. It had sounded like a threat.

"Hey, are you asleep?" Billy's round face peered around the door. "If you are, just say the word and I'll disappear."

"I'm asleep," Jody said.

"Too bad." Billy was speaking in a stage whisper. "I've brought food — soup, bread, salad, Chips Ahoy. I guess I'll have to eat it myself."

"I'm awake now. Bring it in." Jody held her breath as he came in, biting his lip, keeping his eyes on the tray. He made it without tripping and set the tray down on her lap. "Thanks, this looks great."

"I opened the soup can and shook the salad-dressing bottle myself." Billy started to sit on the bed, caught himself, and stayed standing.

"You can sit," Jody told him. "My ankle's against the wall. I don't think you'll hit it."

"No, that's okay. I'm going down and eat with the rest of them in a minute. Sasha . . ." He stopped.

Jody could have finished the sentence for him: "Sasha asked me to bring it up." She didn't say it, though. Billy was obviously embarrassed about last night. He probably regretted it but didn't know how to say so. Let it slide, Jody told herself. She spooned up some soup. Beef barley, much better than the stuff she'd tried at lunch. She discovered that she was ravenous and swallowed several more spoonfuls before she said another word.

"I feel like a pig," she said at last. "Don't tell me I look like one, please," she added. She offered Billy a cookie.

"Thanks." Billy took it and munched on it while Jody ate her dinner. "Actually, you look pale," he said. "I heard we're supposed to watch and see if you throw up." He looked a little sick at the thought.

Jody laughed. "It's been four hours," she said. "And I just stuffed myself. If I can keep this down, then I'll be fine."

"Good." Billy hesitated. "Jody, about last night. I kind of lost my sense of humor there for a while. I didn't mean the things I said." He smiled nervously. "Gotta go," he said quickly. "Watching you eat made me realize I'm starving."

Jody frowned as she watched him leave. Last night, when Billy had talked about hating Leahna and Sasha, he'd sounded a lot more honest than he had just now. He said he'd lost his sense of humor, but Jody couldn't help wondering if he ever really had one. She didn't know if he was really a joker, or if it was just an act, a cover for some very *un*funny feelings.

A half hour later, Chris, Ellen, and Sasha came into the room. "We came to ask if you think you can get downstairs," Sasha said.

"Sure, I suppose so. Why?"

"There's a party tonight." Sasha was changing clothes, putting on a black wool sweater. "Everybody's going, and we don't want to leave you alone."

"Oh." Jody shook her head. "I can get downstairs, but I don't think I want to hop over snow and ice to somebody's cabin."

Chris was brushing her hair.

"I'll stay," Ellen said.

"No, that's dumb. I mean, thank you," Jody said. "But I'm okay, really. I'm not dizzy anymore, and the only thing that hurts is my ankle."

Ellen looked doubtful, but Sasha came up with a solution. "We'll call, every hour or so," she said, putting the phone on the floor next to Jody's bed. "If there's no answer, we'll call back in fifteen minutes, in case you're in the bathroom."

"I don't think you even have to do that," Jody said.

"Yeah, what if she's just sleeping normally?" Chris asked.

Ellen frowned at her. "Just to be safe, it's better to wake her up."

"Right, so it's settled." Sasha picked up her makeup kit and turned toward Jody. She started to say something else, but then she stopped, frowning at the window.

Jody shifted and looked. So did Ellen and Chris. There was Jody's name, spelled out clearly on the glass. "My mother used to get furious when I did that," she joked. "I'll clean it off."

Sasha laughed. "Don't be silly. After we leave, the maid will come in and do the whole place." She turned away and headed for the door. "Take care, Jody. One of us will call you."

Chris followed Sasha, and after a minute, Ellen

left, too, assuring Jody that they'd call. Drew stuck his head in a few minutes later and said good-bye. So did Cal and Billy. Jody lay back and listened to the clatter of feet on the stairs and the shuffling as people tugged on their parkas. The door slammed three times. Then the cabin was quiet, and Jody was alone.

The minute they left, Jody started wishing they hadn't. It felt creepy, lying alone in an empty cabin, listening to the wind making it creak and groan. And what if something happened? What if a fire started or somebody broke in? How would she get out with her ankle like this?

Her ankle was throbbing worse than ever now. Looking for distraction, Jody picked up a *People* magazine and read it from cover to cover. Her ankle still hurt. She thought about taking one of the pain pills, but decided to wait and see if the pain got any worse. If it didn't, aspirin would be enough.

Talking would definitely take her mind off her ankle. Maybe she'd call Kate. She didn't want to get her riled up by mentioning Leahna, but she could just leave her out of the story. "Sorry, Leahna," she murmured, reaching for the phone.

She got an operator so she could charge the call to her home phone, then waited impatiently for Kate to answer. But the phone kept ringing, and after a full minute, Jody hung up. She thought for sure Kate would be there. After all, her flu was only two days old, and Kate's mother'd been sick for a week. Maybe Kate had gone to the doctor. But no, it was so late. Well, maybe she'd had a miraculous recovery and was on her way to Brevard Pass this very moment.

Jody wished she could call her parents, but she knew it would just worry them. Sighing, she flipped through another magazine. Then she drank some water and reached for a book. It was a self-help book — ways to improve your outlook on life. Jody read a little, and took one of the quizzes to see if she was an optimist or a pessimist. She came out an optimist and decided her outlook on life must be okay, so why bother with the book? She couldn't concentrate anymore, anyway. Her ankle was still bothering her a lot.

It was a quarter after nine, and she decided to go ahead and take a pain pill. The doctor told her it would probably make her sleepy, which was one reason she'd been holding out — she didn't want to go to sleep too early and wake up at four in the morning.

After swallowing the pill, Jody snapped off the reading lamp, got as comfortable as possible, and waited for sleep to come.

Twenty minutes later, Jody still felt wide awake. But the next thing she knew, a bell was ringing in her ear. Everything felt heavy — her arms, her legs, even her eyelids. She dragged them open and finally realized she was hearing the phone. Fumbling in the dark, she picked it up and said hello.

"I was just about to give up," Ellen said. "Were you in the bathroom?"

"No, I . . . wait a sec." Jody's mouth was dry. She turned on the lamp and took a sip of water. "I was asleep," she said. "Actually I was knocked out. I took a pain pill and those things are lethal!"

"What do you mean?"

"One minute I was awake and the next minute — wham!"

"But you're okay?" Ellen asked.

"I guess. Yeah, I am. Just groggy," Jody said. She could hear music and loud voices in the background. "What time is it?"

"Not quite ten. Did anybody else call yet?"

"If they did, I didn't hear the phone. Why?" Jody asked. "Isn't everybody there?"

"Yes, but so are about a million other people." Ellen sounded tired and unhappy, and Jody thought she'd probably lost sight of Cal. "As soon as we got here, everybody split up and I couldn't find anyone to see if they'd called."

"You're the first, I think. Thanks," Jody said. "I'm fine, not frothing at the mouth or anything."

"Okay. Well, I guess I'll call you again in a while. Or somebody will." There was a loud burst of laughter and Ellen raised her voice. "Sorry I woke you up. 'Bye, Jody."

Jody hung up and turned off the light. She still felt thick-headed and heavy, and she expected to fall back asleep in a minute. But she discovered that the pain pill didn't really take the pain away, it just made the rest of her numb. Her ankle was still throbbing away. She didn't dare take another pill, though, or she'd never wake up and whoever called next would get worried.

She turned on the light and tried to read, but

after about fifteen minutes, she gave up and lay in the dark again. Restless, she shifted around in the bed, trying to find a good position. She was sick of lying on her back, but nothing else felt any better. Maybe she was just sick of lying down, period. She slid to the edge of the bed and swung her legs over the side. Gingerly, she stood up, leaning forward so she wouldn't bump her head on the ceiling.

The pill had made her dizzy, though. Quickly, Jody sat back down. As she did, her arm brushed the window, and she leaned her head against the cold glass and looked out.

Suddenly her head felt clear as a bell. Looking into the window of Leahna's cabin, she saw two figures. One of them was Leahna. And even though she couldn't tell exactly who it was, Jody recognized the other one, too.

Jody's heart started pounding and her mouth went dry.

Leahna's late-night visitor was back.

Chapter 8

Like a television viewer with the sound off, Jody leaned against the glass and watched the drama play out in front of her.

They were having another argument. Or maybe this was just a continuation of the previous night's.

Leahna seemed to be doing most of the talking at the moment, sometimes pacing around the room, sometimes standing still, one hand on her hip, the other gesturing in the air.

Like last night, her visitor stayed in one place, just inside the doorway. Jody couldn't tell whether it was a guy or a girl; the only reason she even knew the other person was Leahna was because of her hair. From this distance, their faces were nothing more than pale smudges, and the visitor's head and hair were covered by what looked like a black ski cap.

The window started to fog again, and Jody impatiently wiped it off. Finally she leaned her head at an angle so her breath blew away from the glass. Her neck was going to get stiff, and she had to watch out of the corners of her eyes, but she could see.

The argument was still going on. Leahna still appeared to be doing all the talking — or shouting. She turned from the visitor and strode across the room, bent down and picked something up, waved it in the air. White. A piece of paper, Jody thought. A letter?

Still holding the piece of paper, Leahna advanced toward the visitor, until they were about a foot apart. Then she put out her hand, almost shoving the paper into her visitor's face.

Like lightning, the visitor's arm shot out, batting Leahna's hand away. The paper must have fluttered to the floor. Leahna looked down, then tossed her head back. Laughing?

Swiftly, the visitor knelt down, then straightened up, the paper clutched in one hand. Wearing gloves, Jody decided. She couldn't see any skin at all, only the flash of something — maybe metal — that she'd seen the night before. Without looking at the paper, the visitor slowly crumpled it in one fist, opened the fist, and let the small white ball drop to the floor.

Jody could barely feel her ankle anymore, but her neck was killing her. She pulled away from the window, scrunched up her shoulders and turned her head back and forth, easing her neck. Just as she was getting into position again, she froze.

Had someone come back? She'd heard a noise — the door, maybe, or boots dropping — downstairs. Not wanting to get caught spying out the window, she slid back and lay down on her side on the bed.

A couple of minutes went by.

Nobody came upstairs, but maybe they'd gone into the kitchen. Jody sat up, leaning on an elbow, and listened.

Nothing.

"Hello!" Jody called out. "Anybody here?"

Still nothing.

She took a deep breath and shouted again, louder than before.

There was no answer.

Slightly ashamed of herself, but not ashamed enough to quit watching, Jody scooted closer to the window and looked out again.

Things had changed. The visitor was still there, but Leahna was out of sight. The visitor had moved, too, to the other side of the room, near the wall. Just standing there, back facing Jody, head bent down. Standing there like a lean black shadow, not moving at all.

Jody ticked the seconds off — one, two, three — waiting for the visitor to move, or for Leahna to come back. Nothing happened.

Shifting position to ease her neck again, Jody turned her head just enough to see something hanging on the back of her door, something that had been there all along.

Binoculars.

Should she get them? No. It was one thing to look when you couldn't see all that clearly because of the distance. Binoculars would bring it too close, make her really guilty of spying. She wouldn't get them.

Yes, she would. Might as well stop trying to fool herself. She wanted to see what happened next, and she would have watched without the binoculars, so why split hairs?

Jody stood up, steadied herself on one foot and hopped over to the door. She unhooked the binoculars, tucked them under one arm and hopped back to the bed, the other arm waving in the air for balance. It took about half a minute.

It took another half minute to find the right window. How come it was easier without the binoculars? Jody kept having to take them away, look without them, bring them back up without moving her head out of line. She saw a deck, a black mass that must have been a tree, lots of snow. Finally she found Leahna's window.

Too late.

The window was empty.

The visitor was gone and Leahna hadn't come back. Had Jody missed a big make-up scene? Somehow, she doubted it. Even without binoculars, the argument had looked too fierce to end with a quick apology. Probably Leahna had stormed out, leaving the visitor alone. But what had the visitor been looking at?

Jody moved the glasses slowly across the room. She couldn't see the floor. She couldn't even see the furniture, really, except for the tops of a couple of chairs, and books, and a vase of flowers on what must be a low bookcase. The binoculars were great — she could even tell what kind of flowers they were.

Roses. Long-stemmed red roses. Jody wondered for a moment who they were from. Drew? Cal? Or maybe one of Leahna's many other admirers?

Still wondering what the visitor had been staring at, Jody panned around the room a second time, stopping when she got to the spot where she'd last seen the visitor, standing alone. Pretending the visitor was still there, she focused just behind the spot. It was just like the room she was in — a low white wall met by a sloping white ceiling.

There. There was something. A streak of red on the wall. Thick, dark red, darker than the roses, glistening like nail polish. Had it been there before?

Jody moved the binoculars away and looked without them. She could just make out the streak. But could she see it only because she knew it was there? Was it new or had it been there all along?

And what was it? Nail polish, paint?

Blood?

Jody shook her head. She'd been watching too many late-night horror shows. It couldn't be blood. Could it?

Jody felt a shiver run up her spine.

Last night, the visitor had shoved Leahna down. Tonight, he'd knocked her arm away. Not just pushed it aside, but knocked it, violently. What if he'd hit her again, while Jody wasn't looking? Hit her so hard she fell and cut her head? It was possible, wasn't it? And if it *wasn't* blood, why would the visitor be staring at just a blob of paint or nail polish?

On the floor by her bed, the telephone suddenly

rang, blaringly loud in the quiet room. Jody jumped, hit her head, and had to let it ring twice more while her breath got back to normal. She wasn't sure her heart ever would.

"Good," Sasha said after Jody answered, "you're alive."

Jody put her hand on her chest, felt her heart still pounding. "Yes, I'm alive and kicking." She laughed too loudly. "Not exactly kicking, but you know what I mean. I'm fine."

"Good. Were you asleep?"

"Uh, yeah, but that's okay." It was quiet on the other end. "What happened?" Jody asked. "Is the party over? I don't hear any music or anything."

"It moved to somebody else's cabin," Sasha said. "I don't think they've found the stereo yet." She laughed. "There's been a little beer-drinking and a few people aren't seeing too straight."

Jody picked up the clock on her bedside stool. Eleven. "Is everybody else there, too?"

"It's hard to tell, there are so many people all over the place. Why?"

"I was just thinking you could tell them not to call me anymore," Jody said. "I know the doctor said twenty-four hours, but I feel great. Well, not great. My ankle still hurts. But my head's fine, even after that pain pill."

"Oh, you took one?"

"Yes, and it knocked me out. Ellen called and woke me up and at first I was really groggy from it," Jody said. "But I'm not anymore, and I don't think anyone should bother calling."

"It's not a bother," Sasha said. "But if you want, I'll tell everybody. Well, everybody I see," she added. "It's a crazy night, and I might miss a few, so don't be surprised if someone else calls."

"Okay." Jody scooted back on the bed. Without thinking, she used her bad foot to push with and took a sharp breath when the pain hit her.

"Your ankle must be worse than you said," Sasha remarked. "Take another pill, why don't you, and go to sleep. I'll try to find everyone so they won't call and wake you."

"Maybe I will. 'Bye, Sasha."

The minute she hung up, Jody lifted the binoculars and swung them back toward the window. Nothing had changed. No one was in the room. The roses still bloomed in their vase.

The streak of red was still on the wall.

Jody watched a minute or two longer, waiting to see if Leahna would come back, but she didn't. Jody kept watching, almost willing Leahna to appear so she'd know she was all right.

But the room stayed empty, like a stage set waiting for the actors to make their entrance.

Suddenly Jody was very tired. The binoculars felt heavier in her hands, and her arms ached from holding them. She lowered them into her lap, trying to get up the energy to put them back. The last thing she wanted was for somebody to come back and figure out what she'd been up to. But her eyelids were so heavy, and her body just sank farther into the bed, not listening to her brain. Finally she stretched out, covered the binoculars with the blanket, and went to sleep.

Blood. Not one red streak, but a river of it, dark and glistening, dripping down the white walls, pooling on the floor at her feet. Where did it come from? If she didn't get out of the room, she'd drown in it. But she couldn't make herself move, couldn't make herself walk through the blood to escape. It was getting deeper, rising up the walls, flooding across the floor to the one dry spot where Jody was standing. She opened her mouth to scream.

Her heart pounding, Jody lay still for a minute, trying to push the nightmare out of her mind. The room was still dark, and she didn't hear anybody else breathing. Was she still alone? She turned her head, stretched out an arm toward the lamp.

Suddenly her heart seemed to stop completely.

Someone was standing in the doorway, motionless, dark as a shadow.

Jody screamed.

"Jody? It's me, Cal."

"God, you scared me to death!" Jody flopped back down, her heart still racing, the ugly feeling of the nightmare still with her.

"Sorry." Cal didn't move. "I came back to get some CDs and thought I'd check on you." He laughed quietly. "There's nothing wrong with your voice, I can tell that. How's your ankle?"

"What ankle? Seeing somebody in the doorway in the middle of the night took my mind right off it." She rubbed her face and pushed her hair back. "What time is it, anyway?"

"Midnight. The witching hour."

"Thanks for reminding me," Jody said with a shiver. "I guess Sasha didn't find you, huh?"

"What do you mean?"

"She called about an hour ago, and I told her to tell everyone not to bother with me anymore." Actually Jody was glad he had. The nightmare had been horrible. She could still see the blood drifting toward her like an ocean of red.

Cal was quiet for a moment. Then he said, "Sorry. It's been a crazy night — people all over the place."

"Mmm, that's what Sasha said." Jody suddenly felt the binoculars next to her, pressed against her side. Even though they were still hidden under the blanket, she was glad the room was dark. "I didn't mean to sound so grouchy," she said. "Thanks for stopping by, Cal. Go back to the party and have fun."

"Okay. I'll try to pass the word along, about not calling anymore." Cal finally moved, turning to go out the door. "Go back to sleep," he called back as he walked down the hall.

"Right," Jody murmured, already closing her eyes. She heard the door slam downstairs, but she was halfway back to sleep, and it sounded distant, like something under water.

The telephone didn't sound distant at all, though, and it wasn't. It was two feet from her head, ringing again. Jody dragged her eyes open and glared down at it, but it didn't shut up. Who was it going to be this time? She hoped it was Drew. A late-night chat with him was worth losing sleep over.

Jody picked up the phone and heard an impatient sigh. "Hi, Chris, I'm fine," she said.

"How'd you know it was me?"

"Lucky guess." Then Jody realized Chris hadn't been sighing. She was panting. "You must have just been dancing."

"Huh? Oh, right, I was." Chris's breathing slowed a little. "Anyway, I just ran into Ellen and she said I should call."

"Well, you did. And I'm okay." Jody didn't even bother to tell Chris to get the word out to the others about *not* calling. They obviously weren't connecting tonight. "See you later."

"Sure. 'Bye."

Now Jody realized that this party might go on all night, which meant she could be waking up every hour on the hour. She could always take another pain pill, maybe even two. Then she wouldn't hear the phone, and everyone would rush back.

After what she'd seen at Leahna's, and her nightmare, that didn't sound so bad. At least she wouldn't be alone anymore.

Jody was tempted, but she decided not to take another pill. They were too strong. Besides, what was the harm if she lost a night's sleep? Her ankle wasn't hurting as badly now, anyway.

Okay, she thought. As long as her ankle wasn't bothering her so much, and she was definitely wide awake, this was a good time to put the binoculars back.

But the minute Jody sat up, she knew what she had to do — take one last look through the window. She didn't even bother excusing herself this time. She wanted to know if Leahna was back, wanted to know if she was all right, so she simply looked across, started to raise the binoculars, and stopped.

The light was off. Leahna's room was dark, as dark as Jody's. The moon was up, but its light didn't reach into the room. There was nothing for Jody to see.

She felt disappointed and annoyed, as if she'd gone to the refrigerator during a commercial and come back to find she'd missed the good part. While she'd been sleeping, or talking to Cal or Chris, Leahna must have come back. Jody wondered what she'd done — changed her clothes and gone out, talked on the phone a while, gone to bed? None of that really sounded like the "good part." Face it, she told herself — there probably wasn't any good part. Leahna and someone else had had an argument and now it was over. She should stop thinking about that red streak on the wall, too. All it did was cause nightmares.

Jody stayed where she was a moment, staring across at the darkened window. Then she gave herself a mental shake and finally looked away. Her eyes roamed over the other cabins in the row, along the snowy paths between them, up at the sky, back to Leahna's cabin.

That's when she saw the movement.

Not in the window — it was still pitch-dark — but outside the cabin. Something glinting in the moonlight had caught Jody's eye, and she quickly raised the binoculars. She'd gotten good at finding Leahna's window, but it took a lot of panning with the binoculars to finally locate the spot outside her cabin.

Whatever she'd seen wasn't in the moonlight anymore, but something was still there. No, not something. *Someone.* Someone moving slowly away from the cabin. It couldn't be Leahna or her visitor. This person looked fat.

Wait a minute, though. The person wasn't fat, he was just bent over. Or she, Jody reminded herself. Maybe it was Leahna; after all, it was her cabin. Sort of hunched over, dragging her feet. But why was Leahna walking like an old person with a bad back?

Because she — or whoever it was — was dragging something. Pulling something along behind her.

Frustrated, Jody wished the person would get into the moonlight again, so she could see him or her better. But there were trees all over the place now, blocking the light. Jody wanted to see who it was and what they were dragging.

It had to be heavy. The person took a few steps, tugged, took a step, tugged. Jody swept the binoculars back to the ground behind and was just able to make out a big, dark, lumpy thing, like a big garbage bag, maybe. Then the person, moving slowly but steadily, was out of sight.

A garbage bag. Leahna was taking out the garbage. A big clean-up, lots of garbage, because she was leaving for Antigua first thing in the morning. That had to be it. Jody felt ridiculous as she hopped across the room and hung the binoculars back on the door. The big window spy had sat and watched somebody take out the garbage.

But as she got back into bed, Jody remembered something. All the other cabins had garbage cans right outside their doors. So why was Leahna dragging hers so far away? And wouldn't she have at least turned on an outside light to see by?

So maybe it wasn't Leahna.

Who was it, then, and what were they trying to get rid of?

And if it wasn't Leahna, what had happened to her?

Chapter 9

The questions kept Jody awake well past two. No one came home, and no one called again. All she had for company were the unanswered questions buzzing around in her head.

Now, waking up with sunlight on her face, Jody realized that sleep hadn't helped clear her mind. Even before she opened her eyes, she thought of that hunched-over figure she'd seen in the snow outside Leahna's cabin — definitely coming from *Leahna's* cabin — dragging away something heavy.

It couldn't have been garbage, she kept telling herself. It just didn't make sense. What it was, she didn't know. She didn't know why she thought there was some connection between that figure and the argument between Leahna and her visitor, either. But the whole thing had spooked her, and she couldn't forget about it. She'd probably never learn everything about what had happened, but until she saw Leahna again, or heard that she'd left for Antigua, she knew she couldn't let it go.

The first thing to do was find out if maybe Leahna

was at the party last night. She'd gone somewhere after leaving the visitor alone in her room, and the party made sense.

Jody sat up and looked around. It was almost nine. The cabin was completely quiet. Ellen, Chris, and Sasha were all in their beds, all still sleeping deeply, and the guys probably were, too.

She scooted up and started to look out the window, but one of the others turned over in bed just then, mumbling something in her sleep. Jody still didn't want to be seen window-watching. She stood up slowly, taking a quick glance outside — that was perfectly normal — but she didn't take time to really look. She'd wait until she was alone for that.

She was hungry, and her hair felt greasy. Food and a shower were both downstairs. Towel draped around her neck, plastic bag with shampoo clutched in her teeth, she hopped to the landing and slowly made her way down the stairs on her rear.

She unwrapped the bandage from around her ankle and took a long, hot shower. It washed away the dirt but not the questions that still lingered about Leahna. The first thing Jody did when she hopped back into the kitchen, towel wrapped around her head, was lean on the counter and stare across to Leahna's cabin.

Just like at every other cabin, two orange plastic garbage cans sat outside on a little wooden platform. Jody wasn't surprised to see them. But now she was more sure than ever that no one in their right mind should have been lugging garbage in the middle of the night.

It was impossible to see into Leahna's window at this time of day, so Jody turned away and got busy tending to her stomach. She started the coffee and drank some orange juice while she waited for it to brew. When the coffee was done, she sat at the table with a cupful, a bowl of cornflakes, and a leftover muffin. She was just polishing off the last of the muffin when Ellen came in.

"I don't believe it," Jody said. "You couldn't have gotten in before three. What are you doing up?"

"I don't really know." Ellen gave her a tired smile. She looked pale, almost sick.

"Was the party fun?" Jody asked. "It must have been, or nobody would have stayed, right?"

Ellen shrugged and poured some juice. "It was okay. Kind of crowded. For me, I mean." She shrugged again. "I don't know why I stayed, really."

Jody knew. Ellen had stayed because of Cal, because she wanted to be wherever he was. From the look on Ellen's face, all she'd gotten out of it was a short night's sleep. If Jody had known Ellen better, she might have tried to talk to her about it. Or she might not. Ellen was quieter than usual; it was obvious she didn't want to talk.

Still, the only way to find out what she wanted to know was to ask. She'd just have to let Ellen think she was an insensitive jerk. "Listen," she said, "did you see Leahna last night?"

Ellen was reaching for her juice glass and hit it with her fingers. It toppled over, sending an orange puddle spreading across the white countertop. Jody shuddered. She couldn't help thinking of the red streak she'd seen on Leahna's wall and the river of blood in her nightmare.

Ellen tore off some paper towels. "Why do you want to know?" she asked slowly, her back to Jody as she mopped up the juice.

"Well, like I said last night, I never thanked her for helping me yesterday." Ellen's back was straight and stiff. It was clear that she didn't even like the sound of Leahna's name, but Jody plowed ahead anyway. "So I thought if she was at the party, then she hadn't left for Antigua yet, and I could thank her today."

"She could have left this morning," Ellen said.

"Sure, I know. I was just wondering if you saw her, that's all."

Ellen finally turned around and looked at Jody. Her jaw was tight, as if she was clamping her teeth together. Her eyes were rimmed with red, but they were dry. "Why are you *really* asking me, Jody? Why do you care so much? Leahna didn't exactly save your life; all she did was get the patrol. And after everything I've told you about her, I can't believe you really think she's worth thanking. She's not." Ellen tossed down the paper towels and headed for the door. Just before she walked out, she said, "Leahna's not worth your trouble. She's not worth anything, so why don't you forget about her?"

Jody sat alone for a few minutes, stunned by Ellen's soft-voiced hatred. She almost wished she hadn't asked about Leahna, but she knew she wasn't going to stop, no matter how many people got mad.

After a moment, Jody made her way into the living room, where she stretched out on the couch. Maybe she was obsessed, but she had to find out what happened to Leahna, and the only way was to ask.

Cal came downstairs a few minutes later. His reaction to Jody's question wasn't as strong as Ellen's, but Jody knew he was uneasy. His face tightened up, and he stared at her so long she started to get nervous. Finally he asked the same question Ellen had: Why did she want to know?

Jody went through the same explanation of wanting to thank Leahna. "So did you see her?" she asked again.

"At the party?" he asked. He scrubbed at his dark hair with his fingertips, as if he were trying to wake up his mind. "Which one? There were two."

"Oh, I thought the whole thing just moved from one cabin to another."

"Right, that's right, it did." Cal was in jeans and a T-shirt, with no socks. He frowned down at his bare feet, then rubbed his head again. Usually he was pretty cool, Jody thought. But not now. What was the matter with him? It wasn't a hard question. Either he'd seen Leahna or he hadn't.

"What I meant," Cal said, "was that we didn't all go at the same time."

"Okay," Jody said. "You didn't see her then, right?"

"Didn't see who?" It was Sasha, standing at the railing overlooking the living room. "Hi, Jody."

"Hi, Sasha." Jody took a breath and jumped in with the question about Leahna.

Sasha surprised her by laughing. "I thought you knew she's not my favorite subject, Jody."

Jody looked at Cal, who was looking at Sasha. "Yeah, I figured that out," she said. "I just wanted to thank her for yesterday, so I thought if she's still here in Brevard . . ."

"Did you see her, Sash?" Cal asked quietly.

"No." Sasha ran her fingers through her hair. "Don't you remember, Cal? We were together almost the whole time, except when you went to get the CDs. So you didn't see her, either, did you, Cal?"

Cal just stared at his sister, his face blank. Finally he shook his head.

Sasha turned back to Jody. "Well, that's that, isn't it?"

Jody nodded. But that wasn't that, not to her. So far, no one had given her a straight answer, and she couldn't help wondering why.

By the time Jody went upstairs — sitting down again, and scooting up backwards — she'd asked Billy and Chris. Neither one of them had seen Leahna. Actually, what they said was they hadn't noticed if she'd been there or not. Billy said it quickly and headed for the kitchen. Chris almost snarled out her answer. Jody was glad there was only one person left to ask.

Settled in bed again, Jody wondered where Drew was. She wanted to see him, not just to ask about

Leahna, either. When he tapped on the door and smiled across the room at her, she realized how much she was getting to like him.

"Don't you think you're taking this invalid act a little too far?" he teased, gesturing at the bed. "I mean, you could save us all a lot of legwork if you stayed on the couch downstairs."

"Sure, but then I wouldn't get to hear you guys going up and down, just for me," Jody laughed.

"Next thing you know, you'll be asking for a little bell."

"Good idea."

Drew seemed happier this morning than Jody had ever seen him. He'd had flashes of good humor before, but this was different. He was relaxed, loose, a smile playing around the edges of his mouth. It was hard to believe he could ever be in a bad mood.

Jody was lying on top of the covers. Drew sat down and pointed to her ankle. "How is it?"

"It's still there," Jody said. "It hurts, but not so much."

"So where's the bandage?"

Jody had draped it around her neck after the shower. Now she pulled it off. "I tried to wrap it again, but I made a mess of it."

"Let me try." Drew took the narrow bandage from her hand and slipped it under her ankle. Jody kept her eyes on his hands. They were wide and powerful-looking, but very gentle as he wrapped it over and under, finally tucking the end in place. "How's that?" he asked, looking up.

"As good as the doctor's. Thanks." He was watching her. Jody looked away, looked back. He was still staring at her.

"What?" she asked, feeling herself blush.

"You've got green eyes." Drew leaned closer, peering into them. "Pretty."

Please don't let Chris come in now, Jody thought. I'd have an enemy for life.

Drew smiled at her. "They see a lot, don't they?"

Jody thought he'd been going to kiss her. Now she felt disappointed and a little confused. "What do you mean?"

"I mean you don't miss much that's going on," he said.

Jody was suddenly very conscious of the binoculars hanging on the door, and her name streaked on the window. Had Drew guessed what she'd been doing? But if he had, why would he care? Unless . . . unless *he* was Leahna's visitor.

Jody laughed uneasily. "I still don't know what you mean," she said. "I don't see any more than the next person."

Drew stared at her a second, then shrugged. "Okay. How about last night?"

Jody almost jumped. "Last night? What about it?"

"I mean, did your ankle give you much trouble?" He sounded impatient. "Did you sleep okay, were you bored, did you have enough to read, what?"

"Oh." Jody'd been sure he was going to call her on her spying, and now she laughed in relief. "No, last night was okay. I took a pain pill, but they're too strong. I don't think I'll need another one, anyway."

"Good." Drew stood up and looked out the window. Jody watched him as he stared across at Leahna's. His jaw was set, and he had his hands jammed into the pockets of his jeans. Finally he turned back to her. "Better get going. I'll see you later."

"Wait." Jody took a deep breath. "I need to ask you something."

"I knew it," he said, giving an exaggerated sigh. "What'll it be — coffee, ginger ale, something to eat?"

"Nothing. Yet." Jody laughed nervously. "No, really, uh . . . I was wondering if Leahna was at the party last night."

Drew sighed again, but this wasn't a fake one. And he didn't ask why she wanted to know. Instead, he stepped back over to the bed and leaned down, his face near Jody's. "Listen," he said softly. "Don't worry about her. She's out of my life for good."

Before Jody could answer, he leaned even closer, kissed her swiftly on the lips, and walked out of the room without looking back.

Later, when everyone had left the cabin, Jody could still feel the touch of Drew's lips. She'd expected a kiss earlier, when he was talking about the color of her eyes. But when he did kiss her, it was just after he said Leahna was out of his life, *for good*. And he'd sounded so intense, almost mad. The kiss took her completely by surprise, and she didn't know what to make of it. Why would he kiss her when he was angry? She should have been happy, but instead, she felt cold.

Jody pushed the feeling away and thought about Leahna. She didn't know any more about her now than she had when she woke up, and the first thing to do was get the binoculars and check the window.

The sun was higher now, so she could see in. The view wasn't as good as at night, with Leahna's light blazing away, but it would have to do for now.

The room was empty. Nothing new there. The roses were drooping; one of them bent halfway down the side of the vase, only a couple of its petals left.

And the red streak on the wall was — *gone*.

Maybe she was looking in the wrong spot. Jody moved the binoculars back and moved them slowly across the room — the roses, the chair tops, the place where the streak had been. *Had been*. Yes, it was definitely gone.

She lowered the binoculars to her lap and thought about it. She hadn't been watching the window every minute of the night. She'd been asleep or talking on the phone or with Cal part of the time. Somewhere in there, someone had cleaned the wall. The only person staying there, as far as she knew, was Leahna Calder. So either Leahna had come back or she'd left town and someone else had moved in and cleaned up.

Right, Jody thought. Cleaned up at one in the morning, dragging a ton of garbage away from the cabin when there were two perfectly good garbage cans right outside.

Okay, she still couldn't explain the person she'd seen at one in the morning and she didn't know who'd cleaned the wall, either. But she could watch the window all day if she had to. Somebody was obviously staying there, and they'd have to come back eventually.

If only it weren't for her ankle, she'd just go across and knock on the door. There was too much ice and snow, though. If she tried it, she'd probably wind up with two sprained ankles.

The telephone. Why hadn't she thought of it before? This was the twentieth century — she could *call* the stupid cabin.

Jody picked up the phone, got information, and gave the name Calder. It was the only name she had. When the operator said there was no listing under that name, Jody tried to explain where the cabin was. The operator couldn't help.

Jody hung up the phone, then immediately picked it up again. Kate might know. Not the number, but maybe she'd know if Leahna's parents were divorced or if someone else owned the cabin, and she might have another name Jody could use. Besides, Jody hadn't heard from Kate since the first night, and she was starting to wonder why. Before Jody had left on the trip, Kate had promised — *threatened* was more like it — to call every day.

Kate answered on the fourth ring, sounding groggy and confused. "I woke you up, didn't I?" Jody said.

"Jody?" Kate's voice was rough with sleep.

"You must be feeling better," Jody said.

"Why do you say that? I feel rotten."

"Then you shouldn't have gone out last night," Jody teased. "What was it, a party somewhere?"

Kate was silent for a few seconds. Then she said, "I didn't go anywhere last night. What are you talking about?"

"Well, don't get mad," Jody said, wondering why Kate sounded so touchy. "I called you last night, I guess it was about seven, and nobody answered."

"So? I didn't hear it," Kate told her. "I told you what my mother was like when she had the flu — all she did was sleep. That's exactly what I've been doing."

Jody started to ask why Kate heard the phone this morning but not last night. Then she changed her mind. She hadn't called to get into an argument.

"Anyway," Kate went on, "Sasha told me there was going to be a party last night. Why were you calling me instead of out partying?"

"You're not going to believe this," Jody said. "Well, maybe you will. I fell yesterday and sprained my ankle." She launched into the story of her spill, giving all the details except the part about Leahna. "So I was stuck here alone last night," she finished, "and I felt like talking to you." She paused. "I thought for sure you would have called."

"Why?"

Jody rolled her eyes. "Because, Kate, you said you were going to call every day, remember?"

Kate was quiet again. "I remember," she finally said. "I changed my mind."

"Does that mean you've lost interest in Cal?" Jody asked. "Just like that?"

"No. It means I changed my mind about calling every day, okay?"

"Okay, okay." The flu sure had affected Kate's attitude, Jody thought. It was like talking to a grouchy stranger. She decided to get to the point anyway. "Look, there's another reason I called," she said. "It's about Leahna, so don't get all bent out of shape."

"What about Leahna?" Kate asked sharply.

"I said, don't get bent out of shape." Jody took a deep breath, then told Kate about the part Leahna had played in rescuing her, and how she wanted to thank her. "The thing is," she said, "and this is terrible, so don't say anything. But I can see into Leahna's window from here and I saw her last night." She hesitated. Should she tell everything she'd seen? She was still spooked by it all, but Kate wasn't in much of a listening mood. No, Jody decided, she wouldn't tell it all. Not yet.

"Anyway," she went on, "I haven't seen her since, but I decided to call her and thank her. Except I can't get her phone number. You wouldn't happen to know who owns that cabin, would you? Her family, or somebody else?"

"I really don't believe this," Kate said. "You've been watching her through the window?!"

"Sort of." Jody laughed a little. "Hey, there's not

much else to do around here — I'm stuck, remember?"

"What did you see?" Kate demanded.

"Just . . ." Jody sighed. "Well, she had a fight with somebody. I don't know who. Then they left. Look, never mind about that," she said quickly. "What about her cabin?"

"I have no idea about Leahna Calder's cabin," Kate said coldly. "If I were you, I'd forget about thanking her. Forget about watching her, too, Jody. You could get into trouble, you know. I have to go now," she added.

After they said good-bye, Jody hung up, frowning at the phone. What was the matter with Kate, anyway? Since when did the flu cause a complete personality change? They'd have to have a talk when she got home.

The phone was in Jody's lap. She picked it up and started to set it on the floor by her bed, and that's when she saw the shadow move across the rug. It only took a second to raise her eyes, but by then the doorway was empty.

Had she imagined it? Or had someone been standing outside the door, listening to every word she'd said?

Chapter 10

Jody felt her cheeks flame with embarrassment. She'd thought everyone had left! There she was, thinking she was alone, blabbing away about spying on Leahna. And maybe being overheard.

But Jody was more than just embarrassed.

She was scared. Why would anyone stand outside the door like that, unless they didn't want to be seen? Unless they wanted to know what she was up to?

Jody swallowed dryly and yelled "hello" a couple of times.

No answer.

She sat for a minute, straining to hear some sound. She heard a few ticks and creaks, and the hiss of wind in the snow outside. Except for that, the cabin was quiet, like it had been for at least forty-five minutes. Whoever made that shadow was gone now. Unless she'd imagined it. Was she so spooked about Leahna she was starting to see things?

No. Someone had been outside the door, she was

positive. Well, almost positive. To be safe, she hopped over to the door and pushed it closed. If someone came back now, and she didn't hear them downstairs, she'd at least hear the bedroom door open. Then she'd have time to stick the binoculars under her pillow before she was caught.

Back on the bed, Jody raised the binoculars and aimed them at Leahna's window. No change. She watched for a while, then moved them over, to the outside of the cabin where she'd seen the figure dragging the big bag. She wasn't sure, but she thought she could see a depression in the snow, a wide swath like something made by a sled, one of those round plastic ones. It wasn't smooth or even, though, and there were lots of footprints in it from people walking back and forth all morning.

Suddenly Jody gripped the binoculars more tightly and held her breath to keep them still. There was something in the snow, something shiny.

She remembered the glint she'd seen last night on the bent-over figure. She'd seen it on Leahna's visitor, too — a flash of what she thought was metal, like a watch, or a ring. Were they the same person?

The binoculars slipped. The skin around her eyes was getting sweaty, so she took them away, wiped her eyes with the sheet, and clamped them to her face again. Slowly she moved the binoculars around, trying to locate that glint in the snow. But suddenly there seemed to be hundreds of glints in the snow, most of them made by sunlight on ice crystals.

Jody sighed. Maybe she'd imagined the shiny

thing, too. She swept the binoculars up to Leahna's window again. Still no change. She sighed again, and it turned into a yawn. She was beginning to get tired. She hadn't gotten enough sleep last night. She'd take a little nap, then start watching again. Maybe she'd see something then.

But she was almost afraid of what it might be.

Jody woke up to the sound of rustling and shuffling in the room. She was sprawled on her stomach, her chin pillowed uncomfortably against the binoculars. Blinking, she rolled over.

"You snore, did you know that?" Chris said from across the room. She was sitting on her bed, pulling on a pair of thick socks.

"I do now," Jody said. "Thanks a lot for telling me."

Chris sniffed and pointed a finger toward Jody. Her ring — a silver one — flashed, and Jody narrowed her eyes, trying to see if any of Chris's rings were missing. But Chris wore so many and changed them so often, it was impossible to tell.

Then Jody noticed what Chris was pointing at — the binoculars.

Jody slowly raised her eyes and looked at Chris.

Chris didn't say anything, just curled her lips in a knowing little smile.

Jody didn't say anything, either. There wasn't any point. She'd fallen asleep without putting the binoculars back, and now she'd been caught. Chris's smile said she knew Jody had been spying through the window. Jody wondered if this was the first

Chris knew about it. Or had she been the shadow standing outside the room?

When Chris went back to pulling on her socks, Jody started to shove the binoculars under her pillow so no one else would see them. But before she could, Sasha breezed into the room, followed by Ellen.

"We're all going ice-skating!" Sasha announced, and Jody bet it was her idea. "Doesn't that sound great?"

"Great," Jody agreed. Sasha was looking directly at her and so was Ellen. She could hardly try to hide the binoculars now.

Ellen stared at the binoculars for a moment, then looked at Jody. Her expression was startled, Jody thought, as if she were the one who'd been caught. Finally Ellen turned away and started taking off her ski pants.

"Poor Jody," Sasha said. "You must feel kind of left out."

"Oh, no, really," Jody said. "I mean, I do feel left out, but that's not your problem. You guys can't sit around all day and keep me company. Anyway, it's not like I'm sick. I'm just immobile."

"I don't see why you're staying here," Chris said bluntly. She looked pointedly at the binoculars. "You must be bored out of your mind."

"She'd be bored at home, too," Ellen said.

"Right," Jody agreed. "And my parents are away. . . . I guess I just figured it made more sense to stay here."

"So you've decided to stay?" Sasha asked, her

voice muffled as she pulled a dark purple turtleneck over her head.

"Well, it's only for a couple more days," Jody said. "I don't know for sure yet." Maybe she *should* go home, she thought. But she'd have to take the bus, and the long ride would be awful. And she did want to find out what had happened to Leahna, what exactly she'd seen through the window. "Maybe I'll check the bus schedules this afternoon," she said. "Then I'll make up my mind."

"Is your ankle feeling any better at all?" Ellen asked.

Jody hadn't paid much attention to her ankle lately, except to stay off of it. "It doesn't hurt all the time now," she said. "But when I move it wrong, it really zaps me."

"Well, I think you should stay, then," Ellen said. "A bus will be packed. You'll be much more comfortable in the van."

"Oh, definitely, stay," Sasha agreed. She came and sat on Jody's bed to put on her socks. "We're going to eat at the lodge tonight, and tomorrow night I think somebody's having another party. You might be able to hobble along with us." She gave Jody a quick smile and stood up to leave, almost colliding with Billy at the door.

"Sorry," Billy said, stepping aside. Sasha tapped him on the arm as she passed. He looked after her, his eyes narrowed, his hands clenched into fists.

"How come you're always apologizing?" Chris asked Billy. Without waiting for an answer, she walked out the door after Sasha, causing Billy to step aside again. Jody took the opportunity to shove the binoculars under the pillow.

Ellen left, too, and finally Billy was able to come in. He stared out the window toward Leahna's cabin, not saying a word. Then he looked at Jody. "Have you seen her?"

Jody frowned. Why should he care? He hated Leahna, didn't he?

"I mean, I couldn't help noticing the binoculars," Billy went on. "And you were asking about her earlier. So, have you seen her?"

Jody shook her head, not bothering to deny that she'd been looking in the window. Billy's voice was flat, empty of emotion, and it made her nervous. "I guess she left."

Billy smiled strangely. "And with any luck, she'll never come back."

Before Jody could think of what to say, Cal stopped in the doorway. "Do me a favor, will you?" he said to Billy. "Go find Sasha and tell her Drew said not to wait — he'll meet us at the rink."

Billy nodded and left, and Cal turned to Jody. He looked tired and preoccupied. Like Billy, he stared out the window, then at Jody. His eyes were bright, but Jody couldn't tell if he was angry or sad. He started to say something, then stopped. Finally he said, " 'Bye, Jody. See you later."

Jody knew he'd come in for a reason. He'd wanted to tell her something or ask her something, but then he'd changed his mind. What could it have been?

A few minutes later, she heard the downstairs door slam, and a few minutes after that, Drew came in. He had a white pitcher in one hand. The other hand was behind his back. "Are you ready for this?" he asked.

"I don't know," Jody said. "Depends on what it is."

Drew brought his hand out. He was holding a bunch of flowers wrapped in green tissue.

"Oh, thank you!" Jody said.

"Guilt made me do this," Drew explained. "Everybody's having fun, and you're stuck here."

"You don't have to feel guilty. But I'm glad you do. I don't get flowers every day," Jody said, watching him unwrap them and stick them in the pitcher. She sort of wished he'd stay around, even if it was just for a little while. But she didn't know him well yet. Maybe he loved ice-skating. Maybe he couldn't stand being inside for long, even with her, when it was such a great day.

"There." Drew shoved aside some of the stuff on the stool by the bed and put the pitcher down. "When you look at these," he said, bending over to kiss her, "you can think of me." He straightened up and grinned, already backing out of the room. "Bet you didn't think I was so corny, huh?"

Slapping his hand against the doorframe, he hurried down the hall. Jody touched her lips. This kiss had been soft, but it still didn't make her forget the other one, which had been almost angry. She couldn't figure Drew out at all. One minute he was like a storm cloud, dark and swirling and frightening. And the next minute he was sweet, kissing her softly and giving her flowers.

Looking at the flowers now, Jody smiled a little. They looked nice — baby's breath, white carnations, and two red roses.

Red roses. Jody's smile faded. These flowers didn't make her think of Drew at all. They reminded her of the ones she'd seen through Leahna's window. Were those Drew's roses she'd seen through the binoculars? Had he kissed Leahna, too, and then stormed in the other night and pushed her to the floor?

The downstairs door slammed, and Jody jumped. She waited for footsteps on the stairs, and when she didn't hear any, she realized it had been Drew, leaving. She was alone again. Still thinking about Drew and the flowers, she pulled the binoculars out from under her pillow.

Leahna's roses were still there. Two of them had lost all their petals, and the rest were drooping badly. If Leahna — or someone else — had been in there, wouldn't they have thrown out the dying flowers?

Jody spent the rest of the afternoon reading, checking Leahna's window, reading some more, checking the window again. Around four she made her way downstairs and fixed a sandwich. When she got back up, the view hadn't changed.

By five it was starting to get dark, and at six, Drew called. "What do you like?" he asked. "Chinese chicken, barbecued ribs, lasagna, Swedish meatballs?"

"I like them all," Jody said.

"Okay, I'll bring you some of each."

Jody laughed a little. He was obviously still in a good mood. "Great. Where are you?"

"The lodge. It's smorgasbord night," he said. "I went the last time I was up here. They do a good job."

"Is everybody there?"

"I think so. We all came together, anyway," he said. "But the place is packed. I can't see anybody I know right now."

Jody could hear voices in the background. It sounded like a small army. A happy army, though. She heard a lot of laughing.

"Listen, I should get in line," Drew said. "This is going to take a while, I think. In fact, you might be eating meatballs for breakfast."

"Forget the meatballs," Jody told him. "Double up on the ribs."

"Right." Drew's voice was almost drowned out by the crowd in the background. "Later, Jody."

Much later, Jody decided Drew hadn't been kidding about breakfast. It was eight-thirty, and he hadn't come back. No one had. Thinking of the ribs made her stomach growl, so she went downstairs again and brought a package of cookies back up with her. She ate five of them, then shut off the light and looked out the window.

No light coming from Leahna's. Jody used the binoculars to see if she could see light anywhere else in the cabin, maybe the hall, but all she saw was darkness. She moved the binoculars slightly, to where she'd seen the figure last night, and gasped out loud.

Somebody was there.

Jody tightened her grip on the binoculars. The somebody wasn't just walking by. He was bent over, like last night, but not dragging anything. What was he doing? Kicking, that was it. Kicking at the snow and looking down. Looking for something. For that shiny thing? He'd lost something last night when he'd dragged the bag away, and now he'd come back to find it.

But why at night? The moon was out, but so were the clouds, and they kept drifting across the light, making it harder than ever for Jody to see. Half the time she thought the person had gone, but then she'd catch a movement again, and know he was still there, kicking at the snow.

Then the kicking stopped. But the person was still there. She could just make out a dark form, motionless in the snow. Standing there. Staring.

Staring up at *her*.

Jody suddenly shrank back and ducked down, her heart pounding like a drum. She'd been seen. The glass in the binoculars must have caught the moonlight and given her away. And now, whoever was out there knew Jody had been watching everything.

Still feeling nervous, Jody looked around the room. It was completely dark. The moon wasn't coming in her window at all, so how could it have flashed on the binocular glass? She couldn't have been seen. Still, she couldn't shake the creepy feeling that the figure had been looking right at her, that he'd known she was watching and was watching her back.

Enough of this. In the dark, Jody made her way to the door and hung up the binoculars. If they were there, she wouldn't be so tempted to use them. She lay down on the bed and decided to wait a while before turning the light back on.

She was still lying in the dark when Kate called.

"You sound funny," Kate commented after Jody said hello. "Like you've been getting obscene calls or something and you thought I was another one. You sounded suspicious."

"No, but I'm spooked," Jody said, glad to hear another voice. "I've really done it to myself this time."

"What do you mean? What are you spooked about?"

The connection was bad, with lots of crackling, and Jody had to talk loud. "I mean you were right about watching out the window," she said. "I don't think I'm in trouble, but it would serve me right if I were."

"You're not making any sense."

"I know." Jody laughed, a little shakily.

"So tell me what you saw that could get you in trouble," Kate said. "I'm feeling a little better, that's why I called. I'm ready for a good story."

"I don't know how good it is, but it's weird," Jody said. And then, sure this time that she was alone, Jody told Kate everything, starting from the first night she'd seen Leahna arguing with someone, and finishing with the dark figure she'd just seen kicking in the snow. "Tell me it's my imagination," she said. "They weren't looking at me, and Leahna's just a slob, that's why she hasn't thrown out the roses."

But Kate didn't tell her anything of the kind. "I don't believe this," she said angrily. "I call and all you can talk about is Leahna Calder! Why should I want to hear about her? She's — " Kate broke off. "Never mind. Why don't you just get out of there, Jody? Stop wasting your time looking out the window and imagining things."

"Well. Maybe I will," Jody said softly, trying not to get angry herself.

There was a loud crackle on the line. "What?" Kate yelled.

"I said, maybe I will!" Jody *was* angry, and she was glad for the excuse to yell. "But first I — "

"What?" Kate interrupted. "Don't do — " She said something else, but it was lost in the static.

Jody started to ask what she'd said, but decided it was hopeless. She might as well hang up. She heard a click, and the static stopped. Kate had given up, too, she guessed.

But before Jody heard the dial tone, she heard another click, soft but distinct. She hadn't hung up the phone yet.

But someone else had.

Chapter 11

Jody put down the receiver with a shaky hand. She wished her legs could race as fast as her heart was at the moment — she'd be down the stairs and out the door in a few seconds. On second thought, no she wouldn't. Whoever had been listening on the phone was downstairs.

It hadn't been her imagination, she was sure of that. Maybe the shadow was, but not that click. Kate had hung up, and before Jody did, someone else hung up. On the other phone, in the kitchen. Downstairs.

Jody felt sweat gathering at the edges of her hair. Someone was in the cabin, downstairs, right now. She didn't know what to do. Crawl under the bed? No, it was too low for that.

She had to listen, that's what she had to do. Listen for somebody coming up the stairs. Get her heart to stop thudding in her ears so she could hear.

But Jody didn't need to get her heart under control to hear what she heard now — another click:

the door downstairs, shutting click-closed. The listener had gone.

Jody snapped on the light, then dropped to her knees and scurried to the door. It was a little faster than hopping, and she was sure she wouldn't fall. Still on her knees, she stopped at the guys' door, raised up and found the light switch, and turned it on. Back out and down the hall to the railing. A lamp was on in the living room. The room was empty.

Now for the scariest part. Jody bumped her way down the stairs and over to the front door. She turned the lock button. Nobody could get in without a key now.

She held her breath and flung open the two closet doors. Nothing there but jackets and boots. Turning, she went into the kitchen. When she saw the back door, she almost panicked. She'd forgotten about it. But it was locked, too, and bolted on the inside. The listener couldn't have come in that way. When Drew had left to go skating, he must have forgotten to turn the lock on the front door.

Jody turned on another light in the kitchen, and just to be sure, pulled open the door of the narrow broom closet. A broom, a mop, and some bottles of cleaning stuff. It would be a tight squeeze for someone, anyway.

Okay. Jody was sure she was alone. She'd been alone upstairs. She hadn't met anyone coming down, thank God. And no one else was down here. She was safe.

Safe and still scared. Because if someone had

broken in to rob the place, why had they just listened in on the phone and left?

Jody was lying wide-eyed on the couch in the living room when the others came back. She heard loud voices and footsteps crunching on the icy steps and snapped her head up. Then she heard the key in the lock, and the door opened, letting in a blast of cold air and snow.

"Jody, hi," Sasha said, stomping the snow off her feet. "There's a storm coming, I think. The wind is awful."

"I know, I've been listening to it," Jody said. "Is it snowing?"

"Just starting," Billy told her, pulling his gloves off with his teeth.

Chris, Ellen, and Cal shrugged out of their jackets, their cheeks pink from the cold. Drew stood where he was, his hands filled with a big paper bag. "Your dinner," he said to Jody. "Sorry it's so late. We didn't even eat until nine, and then there was a band."

It was after eleven, but Jody wasn't hungry. "That's okay," she said. She sat up farther and swung her legs to the floor.

"How come you're down here?" he asked. "I know, you were starving. Go ahead, make me feel guilty."

"No, I just got tired of being upstairs." Jody shook her head. "Actually, I got scared. Somebody . . . I'm pretty sure somebody was in here while you were gone."

That got everybody's attention.

"What do you mean, you're 'pretty sure'?" Chris asked. "Either somebody was or somebody wasn't."

"How could someone get in?" Ellen asked. "The door was locked, wasn't it?"

Jody looked at Drew. "I thought I locked it," he said, frowning. "Wait a minute." He closed his eyes, thought a second, opened his eyes again. "I did. I remember turning the little button."

Everyone was looking at Jody now. "I was talking on the phone," she said. "To Kate. And before I hung up, I heard a click. I thought somebody was listening on the phone down here in the kitchen. Then I heard another click. The door."

"You're sure you locked it, Drew?" Cal asked.

"Yes." Drew was still frowning at Jody.

"We shouldn't have left you alone," Ellen said.

"Oh, don't be ridiculous." Chris brushed past Billy, heading for the stairs. "All she heard was two clicks. And nothing happened, anyway."

"Yes, that's the important thing," Sasha said. "Nothing happened. But, Jody, are you sure it wasn't something else you heard? I mean, I used the phone in the lodge tonight and there was so much static on the line, I could hardly hear anything else. Maybe that's what you heard, too."

"What about the door, Sash?" Cal asked.

Sasha shrugged. "I don't know."

"The wind?" Billy suggested.

Cal shook his head. He still looked tired, Jody thought, and now he looked worried. "What are we saying, that Jody imagined it all?"

"Not *imagined* it, Cal," Ellen said, walking over to him and touching his arm. "Just thought she heard it, when it was really something else."

Jody decided not to join in this discussion of what she heard or didn't hear. She didn't have any doubts at all, but if the rest of them wanted to come up with another explanation, they could do it without her. "Sorry if I got everybody all worried," she said as she stood up. "I got scared, that's why I came down here. But now I think I'll go back up and go to sleep."

"What about your ribs?" Sasha asked. "Drew brought you a ton of them."

"Thanks, Drew." Jody was hopping to the stairs. "I'll eat them tomorrow. Good night, everybody."

Chris was already in bed when Jody got upstairs. The light was off, and Jody undressed in the dark. In bed, she listened to the others moving around downstairs, talking a little. She heard Sasha and Ellen come in, but she didn't say anything and after a while, she heard their even breathing.

Jody lay awake a long time, listening to the wind whistle and whine outside. It was an eerie sound, and it made her shiver even though she was warm under the blanket.

Kate said she'd been imagining things. Nobody else really seemed to believe that there'd been someone in the cabin. Jody felt like it was seven against one. Were they right? Had she just gotten so spooked thinking it was blood on Leahna's wall that she was twisting everything around, hearing things that weren't really there, scaring herself so much she couldn't go to sleep?

Why was she staying there, anyway? She wanted to know what happened to Leahna, but not if she was going to be terrified doing it. Maybe she'd imagined that click on the phone line, and maybe she hadn't, but it didn't matter anymore. It was time to get out. She hadn't called the bus station this afternoon, but she'd do it first thing in the morning. She'd take the earliest bus she could, and by lunchtime tomorrow, she'd be home.

Once Jody decided to go, she thought for sure she'd be able to sleep. She still couldn't, though. The wind kept howling, gusting and slamming against the cabin.

But that wasn't what kept Jody awake. What she saw every time she closed her eyes was that figure outside, standing in the snow. What she heard in her mind, louder than the wind, was that click on the telephone. And what kept her awake was the thought that the two things were connected.

She'd been caught spying, and then she'd been spied on.

And now, she herself was in danger.

When Jody woke up after an uneasy sleep, it wasn't to sunlight streaming in, but to the howl of the wind, still whipping around the cabin and whistling through the snow. She turned over and saw the gray sky, then got on her knees and looked out the window.

It seemed to have stopped snowing, but it was

hard to tell. Every time the wind gusted, it sent up a thick spray of snow, filling the air with swirling white flakes and blotting out the line between the sky and the ground.

Leahna's window was covered with a film of frost. Snow had drifted against the garbage cans, and only two small specks of orange still showed. The place where the person had been looking for something was smoothed over with new snow.

Tons of new snow, Jody thought, looking at the drifts that curled up and over like waves in the ocean. It must have been a monster storm.

When she got downstairs and turned on the radio in the kitchen, she found out just how monstrous it had been. More than three feet of snow had fallen during the night, the announcer said, and some drifts were as high as five feet. More snow was coming down, but it was expected to taper off by noon. Telephone lines were down, the ski lift was temporarily out of commission, and roads were closed. Brevard Pass was snowed in.

Jody picked up the telephone, just to be sure. There was no dial tone. She hung up and went back to the table, so nervous her hands were shaking. Last night had scared her badly — she wanted out of Brevard Pass.

But now she was trapped.

All Jody could do was wait, and waiting made her edgy. While Ellen and Billy made pancakes for everyone, Jody sat in the living room, staring out the window and chewing on a fingernail. She didn't pay much attention to the loud talk coming from the kitchen, but she couldn't help hearing Sasha taking charge, as usual, telling everyone to hurry and eat so they could get outside and play.

"We can have a snowball fight," Sasha was saying. "And I bet the snow's deep enough to dig tunnels. Remember, Cal, we did that once? Billy, don't make another stack, we'll be stuck in here forever."

Sasha went on, convincing everybody how much fun they could have, but Jody tuned her out. She was trying to keep her mind blank, trying not to think about last night and how much she wanted to leave, when Drew walked in with a plate of pancakes for her.

"You're mad at me, aren't you?" he said.

"No, I'm mad at the storm," Jody said, taking the plate. "I was going to go home today. You're not stopping me. Why should I be mad at you?"

"Because you think I left the door unlocked and won't admit it."

"No. I think you *think* you locked the door," Jody said. "I *know* somebody was in this cabin, listening on the phone, and then they left. So how did they get in?"

"You're really sure, aren't you?" he asked.

"Yes. No," Jody said. "I don't know. Nobody believes me, and it's making me confused. Forget it."

Drew stared at her, his eyes narrowed. He started to say something, then seemed to change his mind and shrugged. "Maybe you'll be able to go home later today," he said. "The roads might be plowed. So if you do, how about giving me your phone number? I'd like to call you, if that's okay." His voice soft, he added, "Hey, come on. I'm not saying I did leave the door unlocked. But even if I did, you're not going to hold it against me forever, are you?"

"I guess not." Jody smiled a little. "Got a pencil?"

Drew found a pencil and paper on the shelf unit, and Jody gave him her number. He tucked it into his pocket and went upstairs, whistling.

Jody stayed on the couch, listening to the others talking quietly in the kitchen. Probably about her and her overactive imagination, she thought. She couldn't wait to get out of there.

By eleven, everyone had left. Jody checked that the front door was really locked, then took her plate into the kitchen. Afterwards she took a shower and went upstairs to get dressed, taking the radio with her for company. This wasn't the Arctic, after all, and the roads might be plowed in time for her to take a late bus out.

By noon, it had stopped snowing. Jody didn't need the radio to tell her that, she could see it out the window. But the roads were still closed, and the telephone wasn't working yet. Every once in a while, she'd pick it up to check, then go back to reading. For a while, she deliberately avoided looking at Leahna's window. Finally, though, she gave in and got the binoculars. But the window was still frosty and she couldn't see in.

Around two, she started to wonder where the others were. According to the radio, the lift wasn't running yet. Maybe they'd gone ice-skating, or to the lodge for lunch. Hungry herself, Jody went downstairs, taking the radio to keep tabs on the road situation. She knew both doors were locked, she knew she was alone, but it didn't make her feel any better. Every time something creaked, she jumped. Every time she looked at the phone, she thought of that click on the line. She *had* heard it, she knew she had. Why did everyone want to talk her out of what she knew was true?

She tried to eat some of the ribs, but her stomach was a knot of nerves, and she couldn't even get through one. She put them away and made a thermos of tea to take upstairs for the rest of the afternoon. She was trying to decide whether to take the radio or the thermos up first, when she heard the door open and the rest of the group came in.

"The lift just started up again," Sasha said as Jody came hopping into the living room. "We came back to change and then we're going back out. Only a few trails are open, but our time's almost up, so we don't want to waste it."

"Are the roads still closed, do you know?" Jody asked.

"I think so," Cal said. "Why?"

"You're not thinking of leaving!" Sasha exclaimed. "Jody, even if the roads were open, they'd be dangerous. You're much safer here."

"I wanted to go home today," Jody said, sinking onto the couch. She didn't bother to say that she didn't feel safe at all.

"Going stir-crazy?" Billy asked. He looked half-frozen from whatever games Sasha had organized. Jody didn't understand why he wanted to go back out skiing. But Billy didn't even wait for an answer, he just hurried up the stairs.

Jody stayed on the couch while everyone else hurried around, running upstairs, going into the kitchen to grab a cookie, going back up. Knowing they'd all be gone soon, leaving her alone in the cabin made her feel more trapped than ever. Trapped and terrified. The last thing she wanted was to spend another evening all by herself here.

"We'll probably be eating at the lodge, since there's not much here," Ellen said as she pulled on her parka. "You can find something, can't you, Jody?"

"Sure, there's a ton of ribs left." Jody took a shaky breath. "Ellen, maybe you'd like to stay and eat them with me. And they have a Monopoly game here. We could play that."

Ellen shook her head, laughing a little. "I always lose at Monopoly."

"I'll let you win." Jody heard herself laugh and realized it sounded desperate. But she didn't care, she just wanted someone with her. "And if I land on Park Place, I promise not to buy it."

Ellen looked at her curiously. She started to say something, and then Cal walked in.

Jody's heart sank. Ellen would go wherever Cal went.

"Okay, we're off," Sasha announced, coming in from the kitchen. "Jody, if the phones start working, one of us will call."

"You don't have to," Jody said. "I'm not going anywhere."

Sasha smiled and tossed Jody a cookie from the handful she was carrying. "If you take a nap, maybe the day will go by faster."

Jody forced herself to smile back and tell her to have a good time. Billy hurried downstairs, but she didn't ask him to stay. She was waiting for Drew. He'd stay, wouldn't he? He'd kissed her; he'd asked for her phone number. If she asked him to stay, he wouldn't mind.

Billy left, and then Drew came downstairs, striding into the kitchen before Jody could say anything. "Drew?" she called.

Silence. Then he called back, "What?"

Jody cleared her throat. "Do you have to go?"

"What?"

Jody took a deep breath. "I was wondering if you'd stay," she shouted.

"I can't hear you, just a sec." There was a clatter in the kitchen, and then he came into the living room. "What did you ask?"

"I wondered — " Jody broke off as Chris came bustling downstairs.

"Come on, Drew," Chris said, smiling at him. "This may be our last chance on the slopes."

Drew gave her a distracted glance. "Yeah, sure, just a minute. What was it, Jody?"

Jody waited for Chris to leave, but she'd planted herself next to Drew and didn't look like she was going to budge. Jody knew Chris would sneer when she asked Drew to stay. But she was too scared to let that stop her. "I was wondering if you'd — "

The door opened and Cal stuck his head in. "Come on, you guys," he said. "Drew, you've got my lift pass, remember?"

Drew reached into his pocket. "You sure?" He checked another pocket. He was moving toward the door now, with Chris right behind him. "I can't find it."

"You'd better," Cal said. "I can't get to the slopes without it."

"Yeah, I remember now," Drew said, pulling open another pocket. "There it is. How come you don't have it on your parka like everybody else?"

The door slammed shut before Jody heard Cal's answer. She leaned forward, watching the door, hoping Drew would come back and ask her what she'd wanted. But after five minutes, she knew he wasn't coming back. She was alone again, and dark was coming soon.

Jody stayed on the couch for a while, too nervous to do anything but listen for sounds. Finally, though, she decided to go upstairs. After making sure the front door was really locked, she went into the kitchen and checked the back door. The radio had a leather strap, so she slipped it over one wrist, picked up the thermos of tea, and made her way up to the bedroom. She turned the radio on and poured some tea into the plastic thermos cup. After a few sips, she poured it back into the thermos — she hadn't put enough sugar in.

Four o'clock and the roads were opening up, but only to emergency vehicles. It would be dark soon, and Jody knew she'd be staying here at least another night. She found a magazine she hadn't read yet and tried to get interested in an article about body language. But her own body was telling her it was tired and wanted to sleep. She didn't know why, since she hadn't had any exercise for days, but she couldn't keep her eyes open and in a few minutes, she'd drifted off to sleep.

She woke up to the dark and the blare of music from the radio. She immediately snapped on the lamp, knocking her bottle of pain pills onto the floor. She started to pick it up, then stopped, leaning toward the floor, her hand halfway to the bottle.

The music had stopped, and an announcer's voice was giving a news bulletin.

"The body of a young woman has been discovered by a ski patrol checking some of the cross-country trails near Brevard Pass. The discovery was made at approximately four-thirty, and police have still not identified the body. The victim is described as white, approximately sixteen to eighteen years old, with dark-blonde hair and blue eyes. Anyone with information is urged to contact authorities. Police have not issued a statement on the cause of death as yet, although a ski accident has been ruled out. Stay tuned for further details."

The music came back on then, but Jody hardly heard it. Something was the matter with her ears, there was a rushing sound, like the ocean or the wind. She sat like a statue, feeling cold and dizzy.

It was Leahna Calder who'd been found, Jody knew it. She didn't need to stay tuned for further details. She could fill in the details herself: Leahna arguing with a visitor, the visitor standing alone, the red streak on the wall that had been washed off, the dying roses, the dark figure dragging something away from the cabin. Dragging Leahna's body away. And Jody had seen it all.

Someone had killed Leahna, and Jody had seen that someone. Seen him come back last night, frantically trying to find something he'd lost in the snow, something that might tie him to the killing. And then he'd stopped, a dark figure in the snow, staring up at the window where Jody was watching.

Jody had seen the killer, and the killer had seen her.

Chapter 12

Still cold and dizzy, Jody reached out a shaky hand for the phone. She had to call the police, tell them what she knew. But there was no dial tone. The phone was dead. Jody slammed it down in frustration and then glared at her ankle. She wanted to move, to pace around the room. Her thoughts were going double-time, it wasn't fair that she had to sit still through something like this.

The radio was still playing music, and Jody shut it off. She had to decide what to do. The announcer said they'd found the body about four-thirty. It was six now, so maybe they'd identified her. Jody turned off the light and snatched up the binoculars. Leahna's cabin was dark. If the police had found out who she was, wouldn't they be there, looking for clues? Could they have come and gone already?

Everything Jody knew about the police she'd learned on television; she had no idea how things really worked. One thing she was sure about, though, was that they didn't just put a dead body on display and ask people if they knew who she was.

So what did they do? Wait for somebody — parents, a friend, a boyfriend — to report that they hadn't heard from her in three days?

It had to be something like that, Jody thought. So where were Leahna's friends? Not in this cabin, that was for sure. Except for Cal. But Cal probably thought she'd gone to Antigua.

What about her parents? Weren't they worried when they didn't hear from her? Where were they, anyway — in Antigua? Jody had no idea. Maybe it was a real loose family relationship and Leahna didn't have to report in.

Leahna wasn't a total stranger to Brevard Pass, though. The police must be asking people who worked here to try to identify her. Maybe some people recognized her, but didn't know her name or something. The police might be using a photograph or a drawing, going around from place to place. That would take time.

Jody tried the phone again. It still wasn't working, but she didn't slam it down this time. She was feeling calmer, at least calm enough to try to convince herself that it didn't have to be *Leahna's* body they'd found.

She turned on the light, poured some more tea, and took a sip. It was still hot, but she'd forgotten how bitter it was, so she set it aside. Then she sat back and started going over everything she'd seen. Leahna arguing with somebody, twice. The red streak on the wall, the hunched-over figure dragging a bag, then somebody kicking in the snow. It could be that the visitor had thrown Leahna against the wall, killed her, and come back later in the night to hide her body up on the slopes. Then he'd come back the next night to search for whatever he'd dropped in the snow.

Or, she told herself, Leahna could have gotten mad, thrown a jar of nail polish at the visitor, missed, hit the wall and stormed out. Leahna could have left for Antigua without throwing out the roses. Like Jody had said jokingly to Kate, maybe she was a slob. A selective slob — she cleaned the wall but left the roses to die. And the person in the snow didn't have to be Leahna's visitor, guilty of murder and trying to get rid of the evidence.

Which was it? Jody didn't know. She wanted to believe the second one, but she couldn't make herself do it. She still wanted to call the police. Let them think she was hysterical, she didn't care. She'd be happy to find out she was wrong.

She looked out the window again. There was no light in Leahna's cabin. She tried the phone. Still dead. She turned on the radio, hoping the body had been identified and it wasn't Leahna. She sat for fifteen minutes, but when the news came on, nothing had changed.

What now? Wait, that's all she could do. When the others came back, she could tell them, and they could go to the police for her. It was six-thirty. They were probably eating now. Maybe they wouldn't take so long tonight.

Having to wait didn't keep Jody calm. She suddenly realized that her muscles were all clenched, even her jaw and her stomach. She tried to make herself relax, but she couldn't. Instead of sitting around, she decided to go downstairs, just to move.

She started to get up and almost fell when her good foot hit the pill bottle she'd knocked over earlier. She sat down again, picked up the bottle, started to put it on the stool. Her hand stopped in midair, and she looked at the bottle. Frowning a little, she shook it.

Something was wrong. Jody started to open the bottle, but her fingers were clumsy with the safety cap, and she bent a fingernail halfway back. She dropped the bottle, grabbed it up again, finally got the top off and looked inside.

The doctor had given her twelve pills. She'd taken one, the first night. She tipped the bottle and poured the pills into the palm of her hand. Four left. What had happened to the other seven?

As far as she knew, nobody in the cabin used drugs. But she wasn't sure. Maybe one of them liked the floaty feeling pain pills gave you before they knocked you out. Or maybe somebody just couldn't sleep.

Jody shook her head and put the pills back, still frowning. Then she picked up the thermos and cup and poured back the tea she hadn't drunk. She was capping the thermos when she thought of something, and the thought hit her like a punch in the stomach.

The tea had been bitter.

She'd thought it was because she hadn't put enough sugar in it. But maybe that wasn't it at all.

Maybe it was bitter because seven of her pills

had been dissolved in it. And maybe if she'd drunk more than a few sips earlier, she'd still be asleep. The thermos held about two or three cups — if she'd had it all, all seven pills, would she be dead? Maybe, if the others didn't come back in time to find her.

The others.

In her mind's eye, Jody saw them moving through the cabin that afternoon getting ready to go skiing. She'd just finished making the tea, and she'd left it in the kitchen.

Nobody else had been in the cabin, nobody else could have taken her pills and put them in the tea.

Only one of the others.

Wait a minute, wait a minute. She didn't know for sure that her tea had been drugged. She was guessing, just like she was guessing that the body of the young woman was the body of Leahna Calder.

But Jody's mind kept pushing on, she couldn't stop it. She'd written her name on the window, and everyone had seen it. She'd used the binoculars, and everybody knew about that, too. She'd asked questions about Leahna, but she hadn't gotten a straight answer from anyone. She'd seen that figure searching frantically through the snow, and later, she'd heard the phone being hung up downstairs, and the door shutting.

Somebody knew.

Somebody knew that Jody had been watching, and they were afraid of what she might have seen. Then they came in and heard her telling everything to Kate.

Drew had been right — he hadn't left the door unlocked. Whoever came in had used a key.

Jody bent over, her head in her hands. She was shaking her head slightly, not wanting to believe what she was thinking.

Suddenly her head shot up and her eyes opened wide and her heart started hammering in her chest. She had heard the door open downstairs.

Someone had come back.

The door slammed, and Jody heard shuffling sounds. Then a fast *thump-thump* as someone trotted up the stairs. Jody stood up, watching the door. She wanted to run, but there was nowhere to go. She wanted to scream, but her mouth was dry. She couldn't make a sound. All she could do was wait.

It was Chris who came through the door. She gasped when she saw Jody standing there. "God, Jody!"

Jody licked her lips and swallowed. "What?"

Chris kept staring at her. Then she said, "You scared me. I didn't think you were awake."

Jody didn't move. "Why wouldn't I be?"

"Because." Chris walked across the room and started rummaging through a pile of clothes she'd left on her bed. "Sleeping's about all you've been doing lately."

Jody watched her, saw her rings and bracelets flashing and wondered again if any of them were missing. "What are you doing here?" That sounded wrong. "I mean, are the others coming back, too?"

Chris's yellow sweater had a dark stain across the front and she was taking it off. She picked up a black sweater and stood there, smiling at Jody. It wasn't a nice smile. "Are you hearing noises again?" She cocked her head, still looking at Jody. "You know, maybe you *should* be scared. They found a body up on one of the trails today. No one knows who it is or what happened yet, but everybody's talking about a maniac running around Brevard Pass. Maybe he was in here last night."

Jody felt her good leg shaking and hoped Chris wouldn't notice. "Why'd you come back?" she asked again.

"Because," Chris said, pulling the clean sweater over her head, "Billy spilled grape soda all over me, and I wanted to change, that's why. Okay?"

"So you're going back to the lodge?" Jody asked. "Is everyone else still there? When are they coming back here?"

"What is this, a test?" Chris was heading for the door now. "I don't know what everybody else is doing, Jody. I only know what I'm doing." She eyed the binoculars on the bed, then looked at Jody. "I know what you've been doing, too. Better be careful, Jody. You might see the maniac." She smiled another nasty smile and left the room.

I've already seen the maniac, Jody thought.

She waited until she heard the front door slam, then hurried across the room and picked up Chris's yellow sweater. The stain smelled like grape soda, but that didn't mean Billy had spilled it. He was a convenient one to blame it on, though. Chris could have spilled it herself and used it as an excuse to come back and see if Jody was knocked out from the tea. Then she would have turned around and left, made sure the others stayed out late. Late enough for the pills to do their work.

Jody wondered what Chris would do now, if she was the one.

But what if she wasn't the one?

Jody dropped the yellow sweater in a heap on the floor and went back to her bed. Chris wasn't alone in hating Leahna. No one in the cabin liked her, except Cal. Sasha didn't bother to keep her feelings a secret. She tried to talk Cal out of seeing Leahna, and she'd come right out and admitted she didn't like her. Maybe it was more than dislike, though. Maybe it was hatred.

Ellen, what about Ellen? She seemed so frail and soft, but Jody remembered what a strong skier she was. And she couldn't forget the way her airy, little-girl voice had hardened when she told Jody how Leahna had used her, and that Leahna was rotten and not worth anything. Jody couldn't forget the way she looked at the party, when Cal had read the statement, *You wish Leahna Calder were dead.* Maybe Ellen did wish it, because of Cal. Because she was jealous and knew she didn't stand a chance with Cal as long as Leahna was alive.

Who else might wish Leahna were dead, wish it hard enough to kill her? Billy. Jody saw his round face, not smiling anymore, as he stared out the kitchen window and said he hated her. He told Jody the next day he didn't mean it, but even then, she didn't believe him. He'd said he was the joker, but he'd dropped the clown mask when he'd said maybe Leahna would never come back.

Cal? Jody thought he was crazy about Leahna. Maybe he'd gone to see her, and she'd laughed at him. Two nights in a row, she'd laughed at him, and then maybe he *did* go crazy. Lost his temper and shoved her, hard enough to kill her.

Then there was Drew. As much as Jody wanted to, she couldn't ignore the possibility that he might be the one. He'd gone over to Leahna's the night of the party, and he'd come back furious. Furious enough to go back and kill her? What had he said to Jody? "She's out of my life."

He'd been so different since that night, the night Jody saw the stranger standing alone in Leahna's room. He'd been easy, funny, romantic, not moody at all. As if whatever had been bothering him had just . . . disappeared.

Jody shook her head a little, almost laughed. Leahna was out of Drew's life and who was in? Jody. Drew could have been coming on to her to keep her off balance, keep her from suspecting him. If he was, then Jody had played right into his hands.

She remembered Drew's hands, wide and strong, wrapping the bandage around her ankle. They'd been gentle then, but they were anything but gentle when they shoved Leahna against the wall. *If* they did. If Drew was the one.

So many people had reasons to hate Leahna Calder, to wish she would disappear. Even Kate. She'd called Leahna poison. Jody had been surprised at how strange Kate had sounded on the phone whenever Leahna's name was mentioned, so cold and mean.

Jody pushed them all out of her mind and picked up the phone. All she heard was silence. She clicked the button a few times and waited, willing the dial tone to come on.

Nothing.

She lifted the binoculars, but Leahna's window was dark. The police hadn't come yet.

Only two people knew Leahna was dead — Jody and Leahna's killer.

It could have been any one of them. During the second party, when Jody was home alone, any one of them could have left and gone to Leahna's. The party moved from one cabin to another, and it was crowded, lots of people coming and going. What had Sasha said? "It was a crazy night." Cal had said the same thing, when he'd appeared in the doorway, a dark shadow that made Jody scream. She wanted to scream now, but there was no one to hear her, no one to help. It was a crazy night, all right. A night for murder.

The next night was the smorgasbord. Another crowd. Plenty of time for somebody to leave and go look for something they'd lost in the snow.

And any one of them could have put the pills in Jody's tea. They were all over the cabin earlier, upstairs and down, in the kitchen and out.

Jody squeezed her eyes shut, trying to remember if there was a time when just one person was in the kitchen alone. She saw Ellen, Sasha, Billy, Drew

. . . what about the others? She couldn't remember.

Her eyes still closed, Jody pictured Leahna's visitor. Wearing black, it looked like, or at least dark clothes. Taller than Leahna. How tall was that? She remembered the day she'd first seen her, coming down the slope with the orange peel stuck on her pole. Then Cal and Drew had gone over to her. They were much taller than she was. That meant Sasha was, too. And Billy and Ellen. Chris? Chris was about Jody's height. About the same as Leahna, maybe a little taller.

Now Jody was seeing the killer's hand. Hand or wrist. A watch, or a bracelet, or a ring. Something the killer had to get back.

Now she was picturing everyone's hands. Chris wore enough rings and bracelets to start a jewelry store. Who else wore rings? Sasha wore a silver bracelet. Ellen wore a gold one, a thin gold bracelet. Was it too small to catch the light? Drew wore a watch. Did everyone else? Jody squeezed her eyes tighter, tried to remember if someone's watch was missing, or someone's bracelet. She had to remember. She just *had* to.

Jody opened her eyes, looked around the room. She was trapped in this room. Trapped in the cabin. If the killer came back now, she wouldn't be able to run.

Get out. She should get out now. She'd go out the back door, and crawl if she had to, crawl through the snow to another cabin, where she'd be safe. Okay, where were her jacket and gloves? Downstairs. Did she need anything from up here? Nothing, she just needed to get out.

Jody decided to try the phone one last time. If it was still dead, she was out of here. If it worked, she'd call the police and then get out.

Jody lifted the receiver. Even before she got it up to her ear, she heard the dial tone. Nothing had ever sounded so sweet.

Chapter 13

The phone was working, but there was still so much static on the line, Jody could barely make herself heard.

"I'm sorry, you'll have to speak up," the operator said.

Jody raised her voice until she was shouting. "I said, I need to talk to the police!"

Another loud crackle. Then the operator's voice. "Police?"

"Yes!" Jody shouted. She couldn't shout any louder. "I need the police!"

More static. Jody almost whimpered in frustration. "Hello? Hello?"

The operator was saying the same thing. "Hello?"

"I'm still here!" Jody shouted. "Did you understand me? Did you hear me?"

There was more crackling. She'd never get through, Jody thought. She was wasting her time.

Then, like magic, the static stopped and the line was clear.

"Hello?" The operator sounded like she was in the same room.

"Yes!" Jody caught her breath and told herself not to yell anymore. "Thank goodness. Yes, I want the police."

"Yes, ma'am, I need to know where you're calling from, please."

"Right, I'm in Brevard — " Jody broke off and stared at the phone.

The line was dead. No static, no dial tone, just dead. She pushed the button down, then listened again. Nothing.

Okay, she'd just go. She probably should have done that in the first place.

Now that she was leaving, Jody couldn't do it fast enough. She hopped across the room, got to the door and had to steady herself against it. Enough hopping. She could move faster on her knees.

Just before she dropped to her knees, she heard the sound in the kitchen, a faint clink, like metal hitting against metal. Jody's heart knocked like a fist against her chest.

The sound hadn't been loud, but that didn't matter. It had come from the kitchen, and whatever it was, Jody knew it hadn't happened by itself.

The phone hadn't just died again, either. The line in the kitchen had been cut.

Someone was down there. Someone who didn't want to be heard.

Now Jody eased down to her knees, trying not to make noise, trying not to breathe. She stayed where she was a few seconds, wishing she could think better. Should she go back into her room or try to get across to the guys' room?

When she heard the creak of the stairs, she stopped trying to think and scooted back into her room. Where, though? There weren't any closets to hide in. The beds were too low to crawl under.

Another creak of the stairs sent Jody scrambling toward her bed. She shut off the lamp, wincing at the noise it made. Then she grabbed the binoculars. She'd hide behind the door, swing them at whoever came in, and run out.

She was just about to move when she saw the shadow out in the hall. Long and tall, moving quickly and quietly against the wall, coming toward Jody's room. Jody stuffed the binoculars under her pillow. She might get a chance to use them and she didn't want to be forced to give them up.

Then the shadow filled the doorway, only it wasn't a shadow anymore. Somebody long and lean, dressed in black. Cal? Jody heard the rushing sound in her ears again, felt her heart thudding, made herself stand still and wait.

"Oh, Jody, you're awake," Sasha said in surprise.

Jody's mouth was dry, and she had to swallow before she could talk. "Yes."

Sasha laughed, that throaty, infectious laugh that nobody could resist. "Poor Jody. You must be getting sick of this room."

"Yes," Jody said again.

Sasha reached a hand up to her head, and then her long hair fell free. She'd had it up, that's why

Jody'd thought it might be Cal at first.

"You sound kind of funny," Sasha said. "Are you feeling okay?"

Jody licked her lips. "I'm . . . just tired of being here, like you said."

Sasha nodded. "I don't blame you. That's why I came back, to see how you're doing."

Jody felt her heart slow down a little. Maybe Sasha wasn't the one after all. She sounded normal, friendly the way she always was. "Actually," Jody said, "I'm not just tired of being here. I was nervous, too."

"Really? Oh, after last night, you mean." Sasha nodded again. "Yes, I would be, too."

"I guess everybody thinks I was imagining it," Jody said cautiously.

"Oh, well, you know. It's hard to think something like that could really happen," Sasha said. "I mean a robber, yes. But a robber who listens in on a phone conversation? That's pretty weird."

"Yeah," Jody agreed. She suddenly realized she was still standing in the dark. She bent a little and stretched her hand toward the lamp.

"Oh, no, leave it off," Sasha said. "I won't be staying long, and it'll be easier in the dark."

Jody wasn't sure she'd heard her right. "What'll be easier? What do you mean?"

But Sasha didn't answer.

And suddenly, the meaning of her words hit home. Sasha wouldn't be staying long.

Just long enough to kill Jody. And it would be easier to kill her in the dark.

Jody felt her knees shaking, and her heart raced so fast she thought it would burst. She saw Sasha's lips move, and knew she'd said something, but her ears were roaring again and she couldn't hear. For a second Jody was afraid she might faint. She was so scared she wanted to cry.

But she couldn't. She couldn't do any of that.

If she wanted to live, she had to hold on.

Jody was shaking so badly she wondered why she didn't fall. But somehow she managed to stay upright. Gradually the roaring in her ears stopped, and she was able to hear what Sasha was saying.

"Well, Jody, I see you've figured it out," Sasha said. "Just like you figured everything else out when you started spying out the window."

Jody hugged herself, trying to stop the shaking. "Why?" she whispered. "Why'd you do it?"

"Kill Leahna, you mean? Well." Sasha leaned against the doorframe as if she were settling down to have a friendly chat. "It was Cal."

"Cal?" What did she mean? Did they do it together? "I don't understand," Jody said.

"No, you probably don't." Sasha ran the fingers of one hand through her hair. Jody saw her silver bracelet shimmer for a second. Sasha must have seen her notice it, because she said, "Yes. I found it, Jody. I was lucky wasn't I, that the storm didn't come any sooner? I must have looked ridiculous, stomping around in the snow like that. Did I?"

"No, just in a hurry," Jody said. "I couldn't tell who you were."

"No. But you've got a busy mind, you would have

figured it out. Once I found the bracelet, I only had to worry about you."

Sasha turned her head for a second, to look out in the hall. Jody sat down on the bed, slipped her hand under the pillow, and touched the binoculars.

"I was going to tell you to go ahead and sit," Sasha said. "You've been standing like a statue. Your good leg must be tired."

"How thoughtful." Jody bit her lip, wishing she hadn't said it.

But Sasha just shook her head. "Oh, Jody, don't be sarcastic," she said sadly. "That's not like you. Leave that to Chris. You know, I wish it *were* Chris, not you. I liked you. For a while."

Jody didn't want to hear about Sasha's regrets. "You were going to tell me about Cal."

"Yes, Cal." Sasha shifted in the doorway, and Jody tensed. But she was only leaning the other way now, her arms crossed, one leg bent. She looked relaxed, but Jody didn't dare make a move yet. Jody sat still, not taking her eyes away from Sasha.

"I love Cal," Sasha said. "We were always so close. Well, you probably guessed that. We didn't have to talk half the time. Our minds just seemed to communicate without talk. We argued plenty of times, but we always stuck up for each other against somebody else. No one could come between us."

Jody remembered something: At the party, when Cal and Sasha were standing near her, talking. Jody didn't know what they'd been talking about, but Cal had sounded sad. And he'd said, "Things change."

Now, Jody said it out loud. "Things change."

Sasha nodded. "I told Cal that Leahna wasn't any good for him. And she wasn't — he knew she wasn't. But he wouldn't stop hoping. He wouldn't listen to me."

"But . . ." Jody knew she shouldn't argue, but she couldn't help it. "You mean, you killed her to get her out of his life? Sasha, there'll be other girls after Leahna."

"Sure there will." Sasha sounded so reasonable. "You don't understand, Jody. I don't want to keep girls out of Cal's life. Don't be silly."

"You're right, I don't understand."

"Stop interrupting and maybe you will!" Sasha's voice was harsh and cold, and Jody shrank back from the sound of it. She wrapped her fingers around the binoculars and held on tight.

When she spoke again, Sasha sounded back to normal, whatever that meant. "Leahna didn't care about Cal. She didn't care about any guy, really, but Cal's the one who mattered to me. See, Jody, he was crazy about her. He actually thought he was in love with her, that he had a chance with her. I tried to tell him he didn't. But he wouldn't listen. I told him he'd get hurt, and he said he didn't believe it. And he didn't care. But I cared!"

Was Sasha crying? Jody hoped so. Let her cry, she thought. Let her get hysterical, fall on the floor sobbing. Anything so Jody could get away.

Sasha might have been crying, but she was still in control. And she didn't move from the doorway. "He sent her flowers. He sent her a note," she went on, her voice calmer. "And then he went to see her after the party. When he came back, he said he'd asked her to stay another day or two. Do you know, he actually told her he thought he loved her? Poor Cal."

What was that sound? Jody tensed up again, listening hard.

But Sasha was shaking her head. "It was only the refrigerator coming on, Jody. I know you're hoping somebody will come to the rescue, but that's not going to happen. Do you really think I'd be standing here explaining things to you if I didn't think I had the time?"

Jody had to ask. "How do you know they won't come? How can you be so sure?"

"Because I told Cal and Billy to keep everybody there, at the lodge," Sasha said simply. "I told them I was coming to get you, that I'd bring you back with me, and we'd have a little surprise party for you. They all thought it was a great idea."

"Even Chris?"

"No, not Chris," Sasha laughed. "She's not there. She latched on to a new guy tonight, and I have the feeling she won't be back here at all. But the others? They're all there, waiting for us, Jody. I told them it would probably take a while," she added. "But they've got plenty to do — bribe the kitchen for a 'get well' cake, find some balloons if they can. I put Billy in charge, that made him feel good. It cheered Cal up, too. He likes you."

Yes, Sasha was good at organizing things, Jody thought. A ski trip, a party, a murder. "What happens when I don't show up with you?" she asked. She couldn't believe she sounded so calm, as if she'd asked about the weather.

Sasha didn't answer, didn't even act as if she'd heard. "Cal told Leahna he loved her," she said, picking up the story again. "And she . . . Cal said she laughed at him! Jody, you should have seen the look in his eyes when he told me!"

Sasha was quiet for a moment, and Jody heard her swallow. Then she said, "So I went over to her cabin. I told her — I *warned* her — she shouldn't treat Cal like that, and she said it wasn't any of my business, that Cal could stick up for himself if he wanted to." Sasha was talking faster now. "I didn't do anything that night. I waited, to see what would happen. Maybe Cal *would* stick up for himself. Or maybe he'd cheer up and laugh it off. But he didn't. He was thinking about her every minute, I could tell. Remember, I've always known what he's thinking, and I couldn't make him stop."

Jody remembered the way Cal had acted after he'd seen Leahna. Yes, he'd talked and joked, but he'd been forcing himself, and she'd known something was bothering him. But he didn't act devastated. If only Sasha had left things alone, Jody thought, Cal would probably have been fine. He was growing away from Sasha, changing. It was Sasha who wanted things to stay the same, always wanted to protect him. Cal would have been fine by himself. He was strong enough. In a way, Sasha was the weak one.

Sasha wasn't leaning against the doorframe anymore. She'd straightened up, and Jody could tell how stiff she was, stiff with anger.

"Before, I could always make him see things my way. But not this time," Sasha said. "And it was Leahna's fault. She'd hurt him. Nobody hurts Cal, Jody. So I went back, the next night. And she laughed at him again. Said he was so cute, though, she just might have some fun with him. She liked his note, she said. It reminded her of the love notes she used to get in grade school. She made Cal sound like a little boy, a toy she was going to play with. And I knew he'd get hurt even worse if I didn't stop her!"

So you stopped her, Jody thought.

As if she could read Jody's mind, too, Sasha said, "Yes. I think her neck broke when I threw her against the wall. There was a nail in the wall, too, but that didn't kill her, I could tell. It just cut her head. That's where the blood came from. Did you see it, Jody?"

Jody didn't answer. There was Sasha, calmly talking about broken necks and blood on the wall. The way she talked — sometimes mad, sometimes as if this were a perfectly normal discussion — was the most frightening thing Jody had ever heard.

"I mean, did you see me kill her?" Sasha asked.

Jody shook her head. "I saw you standing there alone. I didn't know it was you. I didn't know it was you in the snow, either. I never saw your face."

"But you tried, didn't you?" Sasha's voice had a smile in it. "You and your binoculars. I'll bet you're sorry you ever found them."

Jody didn't answer. What was the point?

"I don't blame you, naturally," Sasha said, leaning against the door again. "You must have been awfully bored, sitting around with nothing to do. You must have been surprised when you realized what you'd seen with those binoculars."

"I never did realize it," Jody said. "Until I heard about Leahna on the radio. I thought something had happened to her, but I never really knew. And I never thought anyone here did it. Until the tea."

"Yes, the tea. I wonder if that was a mistake." Sasha thought about it for a moment. "No. After you heard about Leahna, you would have figured it out. Like I said, you have a busy mind. And if you didn't, you still would have gone to the police and told them what you saw. Then there would have been all kinds of questions."

The word *police* made Jody want to look out the window and see if they'd finally gotten to Leahna's. But she was afraid to stop watching Sasha. Sasha hadn't made a move yet, but she would, and Jody had to be ready.

"It's taking the police a long time to identify Leahna," Sasha said. "I'm afraid when I dragged her up the hill, her face . . . well, you can imagine, Jody. There was ice and rocks. Did you see me taking her away?"

"Yes. I didn't know what you were doing, though."

"That was hard," Sasha said. "I never realized it would be so hard. I wanted to take her farther away, so they wouldn't find her for days, but it was impossible."

Without thinking, Jody said, "You shouldn't have moved her at all."

"Oh?" Sasha tilted her head. "Tell me why." She sounded curious, interested in Jody's opinion.

Fine, Jody thought. The more they talked, the more chance there was that someone might come. "I didn't see you actually kill her," she said. "All I saw was someone I didn't know standing in an empty room. I saw something red on the wall, and I thought of blood, but I didn't know that's what it was. Then it was gone. Sure, I tried to see Leahna again. I was curious about what had happened. I even thought it might have been something bad, but there was no way I could *know*."

Sasha moved a little, and Jody stopped talking. But Sasha was only rubbing her foot against her leg. "Keep going," she said.

"If you hadn't taken her away, if you'd left her there, it might have been days before anybody found her," Jody said. "Nobody came to the cabin that I saw. I don't know anything about her family, but they must not have been worried because nobody was asking any questions or knocking on her door. If you'd left her there, we might have gone home before she was found."

"And you might never even have heard that she was dead," Sasha went on. "Who would have told you? Kate, I guess, but she wouldn't find out for days, maybe even longer. By then . . ." she laughed softly. "Very good, Jody. Too bad I didn't think of that, isn't it?"

Yes, Jody thought. Too bad.

"Well," Sasha sighed. "I think we've talked enough now. I should be getting back to the lodge to break the news."

Sasha pushed herself up straight, moved her arm, and Jody saw something flash again. Not the bracelet this time. Something silver. Something metal. Jody remembered the sound she'd heard in the kitchen, and she knew what it was even before she could really see it.

Sasha had a knife in her hand.

Chapter 14

The sight of the knife in Sasha's hand sent a wave of fear through Jody. The fear was hot; she felt the sweat break out at the edges of her hair, and her hands were clammy. But her arms were cold, prickly with goose bumps, and she was starting to shiver. If she tried to move, she thought she'd collapse. She clamped her jaws together and held herself rigid, every muscle as tight as she could get it, trying to keep herself from shaking.

As much as Jody wanted to scream and cry and crawl under the covers, she didn't take her eyes away from that slender figure across the room.

Sasha hadn't moved. She was still standing in the doorway, her arms hanging loose at her sides, the knife pointing toward the floor. She rubbed her thumb back and forth on the knife handle, but she didn't move.

Jody's mind was starting to work again. She felt the binoculars in her hand, under the pillow, and she slid her hand a little until it touched the leather strap. She curled her fingers around it and held on tight. When Sasha came for her, she'd fling the pillow with her other hand first. That would throw Sasha off balance, wouldn't it? By then Jody would be on her feet, and she'd use the binoculars.

What should she aim for, Sasha's head, the knife? Her arm, that would be best. Hit the arm holding the knife and run. Hit her anywhere and run. But don't throw the binoculars, keep hold of them, she might need them again.

"I can imagine what's going through your mind, Jody."

Jody jumped.

"You've been thinking so hard, I can almost hear the wheels turning," Sasha said. "You're trying to figure out how to get away, aren't you?"

What was she doing? Jody wondered. Why was she starting up a conversation again? She'd said it was time. Not that Jody was ready, how could she ever be *ready* to fight off somebody with a knife? But she'd been holding herself together so tightly she was afraid that if she didn't move soon she might snap apart.

Afraid. Maybe Sasha was afraid, too. After all, slamming somebody against a wall was very different from looking someone else in the eye and knifing her. Jody didn't doubt that Sasha was going to try, but she might be talking just to put it off for a little longer.

"Aren't you, Jody?" Sasha asked again. "Aren't you looking for a way to escape?"

"Sure." Jody's voice sounded shrill in her ears,

and she took a deep breath. "Wouldn't you be?"

Sasha laughed. "Yes, I guess I would."

"I've also been wondering." Jody hadn't been wondering about anything except how she was going to get out. But if Sasha was willing to talk, Jody would think of something to wonder about. "You said you killed Leahna because of Cal, because she hurt him."

"Yes, nobody hurts Cal," Sasha said again.

"But how's he going to feel when he finds out?" Jody asked. "Don't you think what you've done is going to hurt him? You're twins, you're really close. What's going to happen to Cal when you get caught?"

"Cal won't know, Jody. I thought I already told you," Sasha said patiently. "Nobody will know. You're the only one who does, and you . . . well, I already explained that, too."

Jody shook her head. "I think you're wrong, Sasha. Once they identify Leahna, and once they find me . . ." Jody's voice rose a little, but she took another deep breath. "Once they find me, they're going to start asking questions. They're going to ask everybody questions, including you."

Sasha tilted her head. "Well, I'm very good at answering questions." Jody could almost see her smile.

"Maybe, but what about Cal's questions?" she asked. "Will you be able to answer those?"

Sasha was quiet.

"He's not stupid," Jody went on. "I think he'll

have lots of questions for you about Leahna, and about me. What are you going to tell him when he starts asking, Sasha?"

"It doesn't matter." Sasha's voice was low now, almost a whisper. "It doesn't matter what anybody asks. I did all this for Cal, and he'll understand, Jody. Don't you get it? Don't you remember? We stick up for each other, we always have. You're right — Cal's not stupid — he might start to wonder. But he'd never do anything about it. He'll understand, Jody, and he'll stick by my story. He'll stick by me."

Sasha was going to move now, Jody could feel it. Her hand had tightened around the knife handle, and she was going to start moving any second.

Jody slid her hand across her lap and took hold of a corner of the pillow.

Sasha took a step. She was bringing the knife up, taking another step.

Jody saw something move out in the hall.

And Sasha stopped and whirled around.

They both saw Cal standing in the doorway.

"Sasha?" Cal's voice was hoarse, his breathing ragged. "Sasha, you have to stop. Please, you can't do this!"

"Don't be silly, Cal, of course I can do this." Sasha's voice was high and singsongish. "You don't have to worry about me, Cal. I've got it all worked out. It's going to be just fine."

"Fine?" Cal's voice broke. "Sasha, you killed Leahna, and you're trying to kill Jody."

"Yes, but it'll be all right." Sasha was standing sideways now, her glance going from Cal to Jody and back again. "It'll be just great. You'll get over Leahna, Cal, you know you will."

"Sasha!"

She didn't seem to hear him. "Everything's worked out," she went on. "I'll explain it afterward so you'll know what to say."

Cal was shaking his head, back and forth. "Sasha, I can't stick by you on this. This is murder. *Murder*, Sasha! Please, put the knife down!"

Instead, Sasha raised her arm, and with a scream, she rushed toward Cal, the knife high in the air. Jody screamed, too, as Sasha brought the knife down, its blade flashing in the light, heading for his neck.

Cal sidestepped, but not fast enough. The knife plunged into his upper arm, and he staggered back and fell.

Jody heard herself scream again as Sasha whirled on her, now, raising the bloody knife again.

Jody threw the pillow and missed. Sasha was still coming at her. Jody shot off the bed, swung the binoculars back and brought them around again, forgetting about trying to hit Sasha's arm, just praying she'd hit her somewhere. She felt the strap slip out of her fingers, then saw the binoculars hit Sasha on the side of the head, heard a cracking sound.

Sasha dropped to her knees, and Jody scrambled around the room, trying to get to Cal and the door.

But Sasha was starting to get up. She swayed a little, but she was getting up. And she still had the knife.

Jody limped around to Cal, tried to help him get up. Jody was gasping, tugging at Cal. He was dizzy and hurt and fell against her. Sasha was straightening up now.

Then there was a horrible cry from the doorway, and Billy was there. Drew was behind him. But it was Billy who threw himself at Sasha, knocking her down again, twisting her arm painfully behind her until she had to drop the knife. Billy was crying and shouting, even after Sasha was down, and Jody knew she'd never forget the look on his face as he put his hand on Sasha's head and stroked her long, dark hair.

The police didn't leave until after midnight. Jody was so exhausted her face was numb, and she couldn't speak right. Her mind was numb, too, and she didn't want to wake it up. She'd knew she'd be thinking about what had happened for a long time, but not tonight. Tonight she'd sleep.

Not upstairs, though. She'd never sleep upstairs. She was in the living room, that's where she'd been since it was over, and that's where she'd sleep. The others were in the kitchen — she could hear them. Cal wasn't; he'd gone with Sasha. No, Jody wasn't going to think about that tonight.

She closed her eyes, felt herself drifting off. Then she felt something on top of her, light and soft. She tried to open her eyes.

"Ssh, it's just a blanket," Drew said. "Go to sleep."

Jody felt his lips brush her forehead, and then she did what he said.

Jody woke up to the sound of thumping. She opened her eyes and looked around. Chris was standing at the closet near the front door, pulling out boots. *Thump, thump.*

Jody yawned. "They sounded like they were right by my head."

Chris jumped a little and turned around. "Sorry. I didn't mean to wake you." She chewed nervously on a fingernail for a moment. "I'm leaving in a few minutes. I got a ride," she said. "I can't stand to stay here another second."

"I don't blame you."

Chris blushed. "I didn't mean to sound that way." She spiked up her hair, her bracelets and rings flashing, then glanced around the room, finally looking at Jody. "What happened was awful. I'm glad you're okay."

"Thanks, Chris."

"Yeah. Well." Chris shrugged. Then she pulled on her boots and jacket and opened the door. "See you."

" 'Bye."

After the door slammed, Ellen came in from the kitchen. "Who was that?" she asked.

"Chris. She got a ride," Jody said.

"Yes, I know, I just thought it might be Cal." Ellen smiled weakly. "How are you?"

"I don't know yet," Jody said. "I think I'm still numb. How's Cal?"

"Well, his arm's okay. But he's . . ." Ellen's eyes filled with tears. "Oh, Jody, he feels terrible. And he can't help worrying about Sasha. I mean, she's his sister."

"How did he know?" Jody asked. She hadn't talked to Cal much at all after the police came. "When he came last night, he already knew Sasha had killed Leahna."

Ellen nodded. "We were all at the lodge when someone told us they'd identified the body, and it was Leahna Calder, and it looked like murder. I didn't believe it at first, I thought it was just a rumor. But Cal believed it. Last night, he told me he'd suspected something had happened to her. And when he found out, he couldn't stop thinking that Sasha had something to do with it."

"Did he say why?"

"Different things," Ellen said. "The way Sasha hated Leahna, the way she tried to tell Cal not to have anything to do with her. How mad she got when Cal told her Leahna was the one who didn't want anything to do with *him*."

"Sasha told me Leahna had laughed at him."

"She probably did," Ellen said. "And Cal said it made him feel terrible. But it made Sasha *furious*. He said Sasha's always tried to protect him, but he didn't need her that way anymore." Ellen was staring at the fireplace, her eyes still shiny with tears. "Anyway, after the night — I guess the night Sasha killed her — Cal knew something was wrong. He didn't know what, but he knew. He could read Sasha's feelings, he said, and even though he never thought of murder, he knew she'd done something."

"Just feelings?" Jody asked. "That's all he had to go on?"

"Well, he knew Sasha hadn't been where she'd said she was sometimes," Ellen told her. "The day you were asking about Leahna, Cal told me Sasha said they'd been together all the time. And Cal said it wasn't true. And then there was her bracelet." Ellen rubbed her eyes. "Cal knew she'd lost it, even though she said she just wanted to give it a rest. He gave her the bracelet, see, and she always wore it. Those things made him suspicious. But a lot of it was feelings." Ellen smiled sadly. "They're so close, it's hard to understand, isn't it?"

Jody nodded. "What's going to happen?"

"I don't know. Their parents are on their way here," Ellen said. "Cal's staying with Sasha, and I'm going to stay, too."

Jody smiled. Maybe Ellen could do Cal some good. He needed it, and Ellen would certainly try.

Ellen left then, to go be with Cal, and Jody went into the kitchen. She saw the cut phone cord and shuddered a little. Then she found some bread and was making toast when Billy came in.

They looked at each other and then Jody limped over and hugged him tightly. "Thank you," she murmured. "I know you feel terrible, Billy, but thank you."

She felt Billy's hands press against her back, felt him sigh. Then he held her away from him. "I can't talk about it yet," he said, his brown eyes shiny like Ellen's. "But maybe when I can, I can talk to you?"

"Sure," Jody said. "Of course."

"Thanks, Jody." Billy kissed her on the cheek and hurried out of the room.

Jody heard him running up the stairs, and heard someone else running down at the same time. Another few seconds and Drew was in the kitchen. He was carrying two duffel bags. One of them was hers.

"You ready?" he asked, putting the bags down. "I called a friend from the lodge, he's letting me take his car, and he'll get a ride with someone else. We can leave any time."

"You packed for me?"

"Yeah, well, Ellen told me what was yours, and I just threw everything in," he said. "It'll probably be pretty wrinkled."

"That's okay." Jody started to eat some toast, then decided she didn't want it. "Is Billy coming with us?"

"I asked, but he's taking a bus." Drew picked up her toast and took a bite. "He said he doesn't want to be with anyone he knows right now."

"How is he? Is he going to be okay, do you think?"

"He's kind of broken up," Drew said. "Poor guy. He loved Sasha, but he hated her, too."

Jody nodded. "I thought he might . . . last night, when he pushed her down, at first I thought he was going to hit her."

"Yeah, but he didn't. I think he realized she's

sick, and he stopped hating her and felt sorry for her. He'll be okay, I bet." Drew looked at Jody, his dark-brown eyes watching her closely. "What about you?" he asked. "Are you going to be okay?"

For the first time since it was over, Jody thought she might cry. She felt her face crumple. "I don't want to start," she said, blinking back the tears and taking a shaky breath. "I might never stop."

Drew took a few steps and put his arms around her. "Hey, I'll be driving," he said. "You can cry all you want."

Jody laughed a little. "Thanks." They stayed where they were for a few moments, not talking. Then Jody said, "I'll be okay. I'll be even better when I get home."

Drew pulled back a little. "I guess you're not going to want any reminders of this place, huh?"

"I'll have them whether I want them or not," Jody said. "I'm going to be remembering this for a long time."

"I know." Drew kissed her forehead the way he had the night before. "That's not what I meant, though."

"No?"

"No." He looked away from her, then looked back. "I was trying to find out if you still want to see me, at home," he said. "I guess I'm afraid you won't, because I was here, and I'll remind you of it."

Jody smiled, remembering the way he'd covered her with a blanket last night, and the gentleness of his hands when he'd wrapped her ankle. "You won't remind me of anything bad," she told him.

He put his arms around her again. They held each other for a long moment, and then it was time to go home.

About the Author

CAROL ELLIS is the author of more than fifteen books for young readers, including *My Secret Admirer* and *A Cry in the Night*. She has also written books for Scholastic's DEAR DIARY, CHEERLEADERS, and THE GIRLS OF CANBY HALL series. She lives in New York with her husband and her son.